APPOINTMENT IN MYKONOS

A Brian O'Reilly Cruise Ship Mystery

Books by Casey Dorman

Pink Carnation
I, Carlos
Chasing Tales
Unquity
Prisoner's Dilemma: The Deadliest Game
Fermentation: Short Stories and Poems About
Aging
Morality: Book One—Where Have All the Young
Men Gone?

APPOINTMENT IN MYKONOS

A Brian O'Reilly Cruise Ship Mystery

Casey Dorman

Avignon Press
Newport Beach

Cover Image: Sexy summer legs in high heels by the sea in Mykonos, Greece by Piccia Neri. Reproduced with permission.

Dorman, Casey, Appointment in Mykonos: A Brian O'Reilly Cruise Ship Mystery—1st U.S. ed.— Fiction—Thriller—Mystery—Cruise Ship

ISBN: 978-0615889559

Avignon Press
Newport Beach, California, USA

To Lai
Whose companionship on my cruise adventures
and wisdom in her editorial suggestions has made
this book possible and fun

Chapter 1

The slim blonde woman stepped from the Florence train onto the platform at the *Stazione di Livorno Centrale*, the Central train station in the Italian port city of Livorno. Anyone who saw her at that moment might have thought that she was a movie starlet, perhaps French or Swedish. Her hair was golden and descended in waves below her shoulders. She had pale skin and enormous dark eyes, hidden now behind a pair of Gucci sunglasses. She had a short, narrow nose and a wide mouth with full, sensuous lips. She was wearing a short, tight dress that revealed her slim, athletic calves, her narrow curved hips and the graceful outline of her young breasts. Her face was beautiful, but marred by sadness and fear.

Julietta Martini tugged her suitcase toward the main station house, anxiously looking behind at the other passengers disembarking from the train to see if she was being followed. Her heart pounded in her chest. Why couldn't she quell the fear that threatened to overwhelm her, sapping all of her strength and leaving her a quivering mass of anxiety amidst all of these strangers? She had taken the same train countless times before, had never felt this kind of fear.

But she had never run away before.

She surveyed the crowd for a familiar face, hoping she wouldn't see one, but fearful that when she did not spot one of Sergio's security men, it only meant that she had not seen him… not that none of them was there. Sergio had been in charge of her safety since she was eleven years old. She had always felt protected by his presence. But now, she needed to elude his security detail or she would never get away.

As she dragged her suitcase behind her, traversing the polished marble floor of the century-old train station with its high stucco ceilings and arched corridors, Julietta thought about what she was doing. She had hoped that by leaving Venice, the home of her parents, and going to school in Florence she would finally be rid of the crushing presence of her father. Just the thought of Alessandro Martini made her shiver in fear. Before she had confided in her mother, many years ago, about her father's sexual advances toward her, she had lived in constant terror. Her mother was nearly as afraid of her father as she was, but she had been smart enough to request a bodyguard for her daughter under the pretext of protecting her from any of her husband's many enemies. With Sergio Magetti watching over her, Julietta had finally found safety. Her father could not touch her with a bodyguard who, when she was younger, rarely left her side.

But still, even in Florence, with an apartment of her own, shared only with Christina and Maria, her two roommates who had become fast friends, she felt confined, stifled, her life still controlled by her father, despite the distance from Florence to his home in Venice.

So now she was running away.

She knew she was not brave... or at least not as brave as she would like to be. She wished she could stand up to her father, demand that he remove the surveillance he had ordered to be constantly present, allow her to go where she pleased, and most of all allow her to be with whomever she chose. But she could not do that. Whatever hold on her he had exerted when she was young still hung over her, like a tight web, inhibiting her every move. She choked back a sob as she thought about what her father's relentless domination had done to her mother... her mother who was sweet and loving, beautiful and celebrated in her own right, but even more powerless than Julietta when it came to standing up to her father.

She stepped into the bright sunlight in front of the impressive façade of the Central station and looked out onto the busy *Piazza Dante*. She could not see the port from where she stood, but she knew that her father's ship, the *Adriatic Voyager* would be pulling into port at any moment. She opened her purse, checking one more time that she had her cruise ticket. It was there: a round-trip ticket in the false name under which she had been enrolled at the University of Florence—another of her father's plans to supposedly insure her safety by obscuring the fact that she was the daughter of one of Italy's richest and most powerful men.

She hailed one of the taxis that stood waiting at the station. In a few hours it would be difficult to find a taxi because of the onslaught of cruise passengers leaving their ships in Livorno harbor to travel by train to the two most famous destinations from the port city: Pisa and Florence, the city she had grown to love, the city she called *Firenze*.

She was getting away. Boarding the *Adriatic Voyager* would be the first step. After that, she would follow her instincts and the vague plan that she had devised back in Florence. Frightened as she was, she felt protected by being aboard the familiar ship. She knew each port where it stopped. She knew every deck of the ship and many of the crew. She would take this first big step: leave Florence and board the ship. Then she would tackle the next steps. She prayed that her courage would not fail her. This was her chance—perhaps her only chance—to find a life of her own.

Chapter 2

The ten thousand dollars Brian O'Reilly had received from Phillip Kramer for saving Melissa, the attorney's daughter, from her Mexican kidnappers just *might* last him the next two months. Kramer had told him that he wanted to be at least half as generous to his daughter's rescuer as he had been to her kidnappers, neglecting to mention that, thanks to O'Reilly's heroics, the lawyer had gotten both his daughter and his $20,000 ransom money back. But at least the fee was an injection of cash, which had arrived just when O'Reilly was getting desperate for such a fix. He was two months behind in the rent on his Hollywood office, and if he didn't pay AT&T and Southern California Edison within the week he'd be using aluminum cans and string to make phone calls and candles to light the office.

He knew that he could relocate to the suburbs or the Valley, where a nice one-story garden office complete with a manicured hedge and a koi pond could be had for half the price he was paying, but he couldn't bring himself to desert the building at Hollywood and Cahuenga—*Raymond Chandler Square* as the intersection had been named—where the legendary, if fictional, Philip Marlowe had had his detective agency. His office was a deliberate copy of the hard-boiled detective's with a small anteroom in which a secretary, if he had ever been able to afford one, would have sat and the larger inner office containing a broad

5

wooden desk, its top scratched from years of resting his feet upon it, a pair of leather chairs for clients, two more upholstered chairs against the wall for any additional guests and a tall seven-drawer file cabinet next to the window that looked out on Cahuenga. He knew that he was indulging the romantic side of his personality by immersing himself in nostalgia for something that, in fact, had never even existed except in the pages of novels. But he still did it.

The area had had its ups and downs. When O'Reilly had moved in during the early part of the new century, the neighborhood was well into its slide into urban blight, and he'd gotten his run-down office for a song. Of course he'd had to run the gauntlet between shopping-cart-pushing bums and derelict teenagers with their gaudy hair colors, face jewelry, and tattoos, just to get from his car to his office. But the cheap rent and the ghost of Marlowe had made it worth it. Then Hollywood had become the go-to place again. Lawyers, CPAs, advertising firms—the vanguard of businesses looking for an historic address and sometimes even a classic revival building from the old days—began driving rents upward. Now the area was home to trendy eateries that provided the high-veggie diet and the California-Asian cuisine that the new generation of jogging, fitness-center inhabiting, low-carb eating young professionals craved. It was becoming the place to be, and now it was costing him a bundle to remain there.

APPOINTMENT IN MYKONOS

O'Reilly was no better at making money than Marlowe had been. Marlowe had given away a lot of his services. O'Reilly was prone to the same weakness, one of several he shared with the fictional detective, but it wasn't really that which had led to his financial headaches. The real problem was that the days of the small, one-man detective agency had gone the way of the hairy mammoth. O'Reilly was a mastodon trying to survive in a world of hunters armed with assault weapons. The larger agencies—North American, Tristar, Martin— were killing him as surely as if he were being riddled by an AR-15.

He still could count on Phillip Kramer and a handful of other attorneys who hired him when they needed something difficult—or dangerous— done. But most of the successful attorneys in town either had their own investigators or kept one of the larger companies on retainer. That was another reason to move to the suburbs where he could work the local attorneys—that and the fact that he was less likely to get hassled by one of the suburban police forces while he was on a case than by the LAPD. He was still persona non grata with the city police department.

It had been ten years since he had been thrown off the force. He'd known he had been committing career suicide when he'd taken that fat bastard, Lieutenant Derrick Sterling to task for hassling the perpetually maligned merchants in Koreatown. O'Reilly had always had a live and let live attitude toward department corruption, even though he had never participated in it himself. In fact, Phyllis, his ex-wife—Phyllis of the beautifully chiseled face, the hard eyes and the voluminous chest—would probably still be with him if he hadn't been so averse to dipping his hand into the cookie jar the way most of his fellow cops—cops like Derrick Sterling—were doing. O'Reilly only brought home his salary. It wasn't a salary that could support the lifestyle Phyllis was aiming for. Her aim was a lot higher than O'Reilly's, and eventually both of them had figured that out.

He knew that Sterling had been strong-arming the hapless Korean merchants—forcing the grocery and liquor store proprietors, the furniture dealers and the ethnic restaurant owners to pay for police protection—and making a handsome profit from it at that. Everyone in the department knew what Sterling was doing. Most of them were doing the same thing, several as part of Sterling's operation. But it wasn't until O'Reilly was called in to investigate a Korean murder case that he saw what Sterling and his little group of blue-uniformed mafia did when someone refused to pay them.

The murder was officially listed as a gang-related crime. Sterling had blamed the *Korean Killers*, the *KK*, although he and everyone else on the force knew that the *KK* hadn't been active in LA for more than ten years. And they'd never targeted women. Of course it hadn't been a woman who'd been murdered; it was a male Korean teen. But he had been trying to defend his sister when she was attacked in back of their restaurant. The girl had said the attackers were a group of young Korean men. She couldn't say anything more. The men had gunned down her brother when he had tried to stop them from raping her. The girl's father told O'Reilly that he knew it wasn't the Koreans acting on their own. He said that he had been told that his daughter would pay the price if he didn't pay the police for protection. He said the police had hired the Koreans to attack his daughter. His son had just gotten in the way.

O'Reilly had tried to pursue the police connection, but Sterling had complained that he was deliberately targeting the department because of his past grievances against some of the members who worked Koreatown. He succeeded in getting O'Reilly removed from the case. Then O'Reilly went to Internal Affairs. It had been a dumb move on his part, in fact, one of the dumber moves O'Reilly had made in a career noted for dumb moves. Nobody in the department, from the Chief on down, was going to cast suspicion on the LAPD for a crime that the victim herself had said was perpetrated by Korean gang members.

O'Reilly lost, and Sterling demanded that he be demoted from detective back to patrolman. Sterling would have won; he had that much pull in the department. But O'Reilly beat him to the punch—literally. He walked up to the Lieutenant while he was in the staff room—in front of twenty witnesses—and flattened him with a single punch. Then he turned in his badge.

He was still paying the price for his temper. But every time he visualized Sterling lying there on the staff room floor, blood streaming from his nose, his eyes blazing with anger, but afraid to get up with O'Reilly ready to cold cock him again if he tried, he reminded himself that what he had done was worth the price.

Except here he was, half of his $10,000 fee spent, no one calling him for his services and his spirits sinking lower than the balance in his checking account. When he found himself in this kind of mood—and he was in this kind of mood a lot these days—he turned to the bottle. He knew he drank too much, but it was the only thing that kept him going sometimes. He reached for the bottle of gin in his desk, then stopped himself. Alcoholics drank alone. He wasn't an alcoholic; he was just someone who drank when he didn't have anything else to do. And these days he didn't have much else to do.

Musso and Frank's Grill was the iconic Hollywood bar and restaurant, dating from the 1920s, which had served the film and literary crowd since its beginning. It was rumored that Raymond Chandler had written several chapters of *The Big Sleep* while sipping gin and tonics at the bar. Faulkner, Steinbeck and even T.S. Eliot had hung out in the restaurant's leather covered booths at one time or another. But it was Chandler and his character, Philip Marlowe who caught O'Reilly's imagination and had made the Hollywood landmark his favorite hangout. That and the fact that they were willing to run him a tab when he wasn't quite up to snuff on his cash flow. He would pay Joey, the grill's bartender of almost forty years, a visit, pay off his bill and have a few—or maybe more than a few—gin and tonics, and remind himself that even Marlowe had had his down moments. He stuck his cell phone into his pocket and started toward the door.

The cell phone rang before he made it to the doorway. He pulled it back out and looked at the number. The caller ID listed a lengthy number, one from somewhere outside the country. It was probably somebody wanting to sell him a condo in Egypt, or tell him that they'd like his bank account number so they could transfer their dead uncle's millions into it from a bank in Nigeria. He didn't know anyone outside of the United States did he? Ted Firestone? Ted was a cruise ship captain somewhere in Europe. Maybe... he answered the phone.

It was Ted Firestone.

"Where the hell are you?" O'Reilly asked.

"Rome."

"Italy?"

"And you said you didn't pay attention during high school geography class."

"That was you. I'm the one who remembered that Paris was in France. So you're in Rome. Are you calling just to make me jealous?"

"I need your help."

"Great, I was just going out for lunch. I'll drop by Rome on my way. How can I help you all

11

the way from LA?" Ted Firestone was his oldest and closest friend. They'd gone to high school together, sailed together since they were kids. Ted had been his high school's quarterback, and O'Reilly had been his tall and rangy speed demon wide receiver. Ted had stuck with the sea, going to the US Merchant Marine Academy and then working his way up through the ranks with various cruise lines until he finally landed his own command with an Italian line at the incredibly young age of 40. That was a year ago. O'Reilly hadn't seen his friend since five years ago, during the time that Firestone had been First Officer on a ship that cruised from LA to Hawaii. They had always needled each other, but O'Reilly would do anything to help his best friend. What could he possibly want from him when he was this far away?

"I need you to come to Barcelona."

"Barcelona? Spain?"

"You really do know your geography."

"I told you so. I also know that Spain's just about as far away as Italy. What's going on?"

"I need a detective... one that I can trust. That's you, buddy." Ted's voice had become serious.

"Are you in trouble?"

"Not me, Well not yet anyway. We had a disappearance. The line's owner's daughter. Off of my ship."

"She fell off your ship?"

"She didn't fall off, you idiot, she's disappeared, been kidnapped."

"The daughter of the ship owner? That super rich semi-Mafia Don who owns your cruise line plus an Italian basketball team and half the banks in the country?"

"Alessandro Martini. And he only owns one bank—with a lot of branches."

"But he must have a lot of clout with the Italian authorities. Can't they find his kid?"

"The authorities haven't been informed. Imagine the publicity if the owner of a cruise line's daughter goes missing from one of his own cruise ships. There have been six young women missing from other cruise lines just this season. He's been advertising that his ships are the safest in the world. This would ruin his business. He's got his own security men, and they're combing the ship like ants on a box of sugar, but they haven't found zip so far. Martini has threatened me with losing my job if she isn't found."

"Holy shit, bro, why you?

"It's my ship. She went missing while I was in command."

O'Reilly sat back down. His friend really was in trouble. "What did you mean that six women had already gone missing from cruise ships this year?"

"Somebody's snatching young women when they go ashore on excursions. It's happened on every line but ours so far. They've only found one of the girls. She turned up dead in a Hungarian brothel."

"Holy shit. How come that hasn't been in the papers over here?"

"The cruise ships don't want it known. It would kill their business. They pay the families huge sums to keep quiet about it. But everyone within the industry knows."

"And you think I can help?"

"You're the best. And I trust you."

"My Italian's a little rusty. Once I'm past pizza and cannoli I'm pretty limited."

"You don't have to speak Italian. Everyone on the ship speaks English. You can get by in Italy without knowing Italian."

"Great. How's that going to help me in Barcelona? And why again, am I going there instead of to Rome?"

"Because my ship is leaving Rome in an hour and I'll be in Barcelona in a few days. I want you to meet the ship there."

He was doing calculations in his mind. "I'm a little short of cash. I've got enough to get there, but I also have to cover my office expenses while I'm gone."

"The cruise line will pay. I've cleared it with the owner. He just wants his daughter back. I told him you were the best detective in America. They think America has the best of everything, so that makes you the best detective in the world."

"Good, then you didn't have to lie. Does that mean he'll pay me my well-deserved world-class fee?"

"If you deliver. If not, at least you've got your expenses covered and I'll pay your fee... at your regular rate. Of course it will be coming out of my final paycheck."

"Forget it. I could use a European vacation anyway. I'll be waiting for you with castanets in Barcelona. What's the name of your ship?"

"The *Adriatic Voyager*. I knew I could count on you."

"Ciao. See I've learned some of the lingo already. "

Chapter 3

Dmitri Dragic looked in the mirror and adjusted his tie. The collar of the shirt he'd worn three days in a row was dark with dirt, but as long as he cinched up his tie, no one would notice. At least he had finally stopped sweating. He was back home; he had almost been forgiven, and now all he had to do was find a way to get back at those two goons, Goran and Filip, and stay in the good graces of Bratislav Vucovic. He didn't think it had been fair that Vucovic had punished him in the first place. Everyone makes mistakes and the kind of mistake he had made could be made by anyone. The real mistake was that neither of those two morons had told him that giving the girls a second dose of the tranquilizer could kill them. Why hadn't Vucovic punished *them* for forgetting to tell him *that?*

He looked in the mirror, admiring himself. He could see why the girls had a hard time resisting him. And Vucovic ought to recognize that his good looks meant that Dmitri could do things that none of the other members of the gang could do. He'd proved that by bringing the two girls back from Naples.

He'd hated being sent to Naples. He hated Vucovic for sending him. Naples was the center of activity for the *Camorra*, the criminal families who controlled both crime and politics in *Campania*, the area of southern Italy that stretched from Naples to

16

Salerno. There were over a hundred active *Camorra* families, often feuding among themselves and always jealously protecting their territory from outside interlopers. Even the Sicilian *Mafia* steered clear of *Camorra* turf.

And Vucovic had sent him into *Camorra* territory to bring back a girl… or more than one. Every time he thought about it he got angry all over again. Why was *he* always the one who had to do the dirty stuff?

He'd had no choice but to go. He wasn't being sent because he was the bravest, or the smartest, or the most skilled member of the prostitution ring run by Bratislav Vucovic. He wasn't even being sent because he was the only one, with his good looks, who could lure an innocent girl off the street. He was being sent because he had screwed up. *But it wasn't fair*, he kept telling himself. How was he supposed to know that two doses of the drug they usually gave the girls to keep them docile would kill them? He'd just thought that if one injection was good, two would be better. Then the two girls he had been in charge of would sleep while he could go out and drink with his friends. When he returned he was horrified, then scared out of his wits to find that both of the girls were dead.

There was no way he was able to conceal it from Vucovic.

Dmitri had at first lied and said that the girls must have given themselves an extra dose. After all, they had become addicted to the stuff, hadn't they? Then he'd blamed it on Filip and Goran. That

17

wasn't really a lie. They should have told him what would happen. But Vucovic still blamed him. He always blamed Dmitri. He had even appealed to his uncles, who had gotten him the job with Vucovic. But they had told him that it was his problem and he had to deal with it himself. Finally he had pleaded, tears in his eyes, crawling on the floor like a baby. All that had gotten him was a beating from Goran and Filip, both of whom called him a "sissy girl" for crying. Those two would pay for that he told himself. But then he had made his big mistake: he had offered to find more girls to replace the ones who'd died. Vucovic had taken him up on the offer. With a cruel smile on his face, the boss had sent him to Naples.

Dmitri had complained. He said he could find two girls in Budapest within a day. But Vucovic had said he didn't want any more trouble with the *Rendőrség*, the Hungarian National Police, who were under pressure from the government to crack down on prostitution. Vucovic had told him to go to the *Camorra* in Naples and get their help. In the past, they had offered to send girls north; they just wanted to be paid for procuring the young women. Vucovic told Dmitri to promise to pay them, and he'd worry about coming up with the money later… when they had the girls. Was Vucovic crazy? There was no way that Dmitri was going to make such an offer to the *Camorra*. He'd just lie and tell Vucovic that the *Camorra* had refused the deal.

But he still had to get the girls.

APPOINTMENT IN MYKONOS

It had been his own idea to join the crew of a cruise ship and kidnap one or two girls off the boat. It was something he had thought of on his own. He was proud of himself for coming up with such a brilliant plan. He wouldn't be trolling for women in the middle of *Camorra* territory, and he could enjoy himself on a cruise. He'd had a friend who had been a waiter on a cruise ship and the friend had told him that the crew did nothing but party. And the ship was full of good-looking girls. Not the ugly whores that worked for Vucovic, but pretty girls, most of them members of the crew; but also there were young, rich girls who were passengers on the cruise ship. And sometimes they too partied with the crew.

It was a foolproof plan. When he saw an ad for waiters on the *Adriatic Voyager*, he flew to Malaga and presented himself as an experienced waiter, fluent in English, willing to go anywhere. Of course it was mostly a lie. He could speak English. It was necessary in his business. And he *had* worked as a busboy at one of the downtown Budapest hotel restaurants for a while—until he had been fired for stealing the foreigners' lavish tips before the waiters could collect them. But best of all, he knew that the *Adriatic Voyager* stopped in Naples, where he could get back off again, taking the girls with him and nobody would be the wiser.

The cruise ship had been a blast. It was easy to get out of working too hard and everything he'd heard about the girls on board a cruise ship was true. And he could tell they all fell for him. But

19

most of all, it kept him out of *Camorra* territory, at least until the ship docked in Naples. Since that was where he had his connections to get back to Budapest, he'd known that he had to find his victims before the ship arrived in Naples. And he'd found them.

The mousey waitress on the *Adriatic Voyager* had been a pushover. Dmitri admired himself in the mirror. He knew that he was good looking, with his slim waist, his dark, wavy hair, which he kept trimmed in order to look more like a businessman—which of course was what he was going to be someday, maybe running a brothel of his own—and his handsome face. And he could smooth talk anyone, particularly girls. Except that rich bitch on the ship. Sure, she had acted nice to him, but he could tell that she'd been faking.

But for sure she was rich…. rich enough to convince him that he wasn't going to bring back just the mousey little waitress. He was going to go for something higher class. His roommate on the ship had told him that Julietta, that was the rich girl's name, was the daughter of the man who owned the whole cruise line… one of the richest men in Italy. Of course if he kidnapped her Vucovic would probably be pissed off. If it ever got out that one of his gang had snatched the daughter of Alessandro Martini right beneath the eyes of the *Camorra*, right in the middle of the *Campania*, they'd all be dead. There were even rumors that Martini and the *Camorra* had an agreement, that the *Camorra*

20

used his banks to launder their money. But how would the *Camorra* know who had taken the girl?

Dmitri wasn't going to bring back only Marina.

It had taken some fast-talking on his part, but that was what he was good at. He could convince a chick of almost anything. And it hadn't been that hard to talk Marina into approaching her rich friend and asking her to come with them to Budapest. The friend might have been rich and she had high and mighty airs, as if she thought she was better than Dmitri, but she was as dumb as Marina. She didn't need a job, of course, so he told her about the party life in Budapest. He didn't have to lie. The city was a destination for partiers from all over Europe. The snobby girl had been thrilled when she heard about Budapest's *ruin pubs*, the clubs that were located in bombed-out buildings that had never been fully rehabilitated after the Soviet occupation. Some of them were enormous, with rock bands blaring music from   several different floors and hundreds of customers partying until three or four in the morning. And she wanted a break from her parents and her school. He promised her a quick trip to Hungary, some introductions to some friends who liked to party, and she could be back before the end of the weekend.

What a dumb broad.

So now he was back... with the two girls. And Vucovic had forgiven him... more or less. He still was treated like a lowly junior member of the gang by Goran and Filip and even Bratislav himself, but at least they didn't threaten him anymore.

And he was finally away from the feared *Camorra*. Reluctantly, he tore himself away from his image in the mirror. He might not be the brightest member of the gang, but he knew that he was the best looking. And, if they wanted to gain access to more girls, they needed him.

Chapter 4

The piers at the foot of *La Rambla*, Barcelona's broad central pedestrian Boulevard, were as crowded as Disneyland at Christmas break. When passengers weren't embarking or disembarking from the cruise ships or riding in one of the blue buses that shuttled in a constant stream between the cruise ship terminals and the *Monumento a Colon*, the 175 foot tall statue of Christopher Columbus that towered over the harbor, they were visiting *Port Vell*, the dock area that had gone through a renewal project for the '92 Olympics and now was one of the main tourist shopping destinations in the city. The terminals themselves were a beehive of activity as trucks thundered onto the wooden docks bringing supplies to be loaded onto one of the six or seven of the ships that were always in port.

Most of the city's hotels were located around *La Rambla*, a street that resembled more a carnival midway than a city thoroughfare. Only foot traffic was allowed on the broad wide center strip that was bordered by streets on either side. Vendors displayed their trinkets on blankets spread out on the cobblestones or in brightly colored wooden stalls. Street mimes posed as human statues, only moving—to everyone's startled delight—when someone dropped a bill or a coin in the box in front of them. On one side of *La Rambla* was the *Barri Gothic*, the old section of the city, with its ancient cathedrals, such as *Le Seu,* whose Gothic spires soared more than two-hundred feet into the air and its narrow streets, often not wide enough for a car, forming a labyrinth of tunnel-like passageways between the old buildings towering on either side of them. On the other side of *La Rambla* was the *Boqueria*, the covered market, where the best meats, fruits, vegetables and cheeses in the city were sold.

O'Reilly preferred the more residential *Gracia* neighborhood where his hotel was located, home to countless galleries, cafes, artist's studios and wine and cheese shops. In addition to the ubiquitous tapas bars, the area was home to ethnic restaurants representing every culture: Turkish, Lebanese, Japanese, Italian, Greek as well as his own country's contribution to international cuisine, McDonald's and KFC. Around the corner from the Metro station near his hotel he had found *Carrer d'Asturies*, a street that was filled with local pedestrians at all hours, but especially in the evening when people came out to eat and drink. The narrow street had all the festive air of *La Rambla*, but without the tourists. Tapas bars and restaurants were filled with people sitting and eating, drinking and talking. Street musicians played jazz and folk music on the corners. Everyone seemed to be happy and friendly. His lack of Spanish was only a minor hindrance as waiters and vendors made their best efforts to converse in broken English with the tall, broad-shouldered American with the infectious grin. Just sitting at a bar with a gin and tonic and a plate of olives and cheese, he was entertained until late into the evening watching the passersby. It was a city he could learn to enjoy.

He'd been in the city for two days, waiting for the *Adriatic Voyager's* arrival. Ted Firestone had kept in touch by cell phone during his stay in the Spanish city. The girl hadn't been found. The consensus among the ship owner's security staff was that his daughter had been abducted. Captain Firestone concurred. She was the seventh in the string of abductions of young women from European cruise ships. This time though, the kidnappers hadn't known whom they were abducting or they would have tried to secure a ransom from her father, one of the richest men in Italy.

The whole situation smelled of something rotten—dead fish crossed O'Reilly's mind, but maybe that was because he was near the harbor. Human traffickers rarely took anyone who might be well-connected, even if the connection was just caring parents. The last two things traffickers wanted were either publicity or gigantic manhunts for their victims. Of course they didn't get any publicity in the cases of these missing girls, since the cruise lines kept the abductions hushed up. But would a gang of traffickers rely on something like that? There must be a lot more young women wandering Europe who had no family ties and would make much easier targets than well-to-do cruise passengers. If this were Hollywood, they'd just have to go to the city streets to find a host of runaway teens whom nobody seemed to care about.

APPOINTMENT IN MYKONOS

But he didn't need to worry about the six other young women who had been abducted… only this one. He'd googled Alessandro Martini while he'd sat in a tiny tapas bar with Wi-Fi, eating shrimps on bread and olives soaked in oil and downing *Mojitos*, the sweet rum drinks that seemed to be a favorite of Barcelonans. Alessandro Martini had started his career as a gambler. He'd come from a poor background, but had learned to play cards at a young age. In the casinos around Venice and San Remo the young Martini had turned that talent into a modest living. He'd also engaged in private games, playing high stakes poker with wealthy men who liked the challenge of competing against a professional, but didn't want to do it in the spotlight of one of the high profile casinos. In one of these private card games he'd won a small family-owned bank from the dissolute and intemperate young man who'd just inherited it from his deceased father.

Martini had turned out to have the same flair for banking that he'd had for gambling. Using a series of leveraged buyouts to gobble up every small struggling bank available, he'd turned his holdings into one large chain under the aegis of his own bank. With money now to spare, Martini was soon investing in everything from steel plants to vineyards and finally to tourism, his country's largest business. His biggest investment was the Seven Seas Cruise Line. He had also acquired *Martini Venezia*, a team in the *Lega Basket Serie*, the Italian basketball league. Although Alessandro

26

Martini had become a powerful and respected businessman in Italy, he was rumored to have maintained his ties with several of the Italian Mafia he had known from his gambling days and who now were heavily involved in the legalized gambling that had swept the country since deregulation of the gaming industry in the '90s.

Martini's wife, although a former model of mixed German and Italian heritage and a woman who was known throughout the country for her beauty, was a reputedly neurotic recluse, now in her mid-forties, who was seldom seen in public. They had one child—Julietta—who had gone to private schools in Venice, where the family lived and then to the University of Florence, where she was studying literature. She was 19 years old.

According to Ted Firestone, Julietta had disappeared five days ago, presumably while the *Adriatic Voyager* had been docked in Naples. The day and location when she was last seen were approximate because she had been come aboard the ship in Livorno, near Florence, under an assumed name, without her father's knowledge, and she had only been noticed to be missing after the ship had left Naples and was on its way to Venice, its final destination before turning around to return to Barcelona.

O'Reilly had hunted a lot of missing persons... but never in Europe. Still, he was finding that people were people. *La Rambla* was teeming with tourists, just as was Sunset Boulevard. He'd had no difficulty spotting the pickpockets and hustlers who preyed on the out-of-town visitors, either downtown or around the harbor. With his muscular physique and rugged looks, the hustlers, even those who recognized him as a tourist, left him alone.

With interest he noticed the relative absence of homeless people, both in the tourist areas and in the *Gracia* neighborhood around his hotel—unlike American cities, where they seemed to be everywhere. Maybe it wasn't so easy for human traffickers to find stray women on the streets of Europe after all… although there was no dearth of beautiful young Spanish women walking around, apparently unattached. As soon as he'd scanned an area for potential points of danger and for easy exits in case of trouble, the beautiful women were the next item he looked for.

Ted Firestone had better get him out of Barcelona before he got himself into trouble.

On the morning of the his third day, in the brilliant light of a June Mediterranean sun, he disembarked from the metro at the intersection of *La Rambla* and *Passeig de Gracia* and took a few moments to savor one last look at the magnificent façade of *Casa Battlo*, the creation of Barcelona's famed modernist architect, Antonio Gaudi. The building, with its wavy, colorful lines, its roof that looked like the back of some gigantic marine creature, reminded O'Reilly of something out of a Dr. Seuss book. It was his favorite among the other Gaudi buildings, such as the still unfinished cathedral, *Sagrada Familia*, with its soaring pinnacles and even the lyrical *Parc Guell,* the city park high on a hill overlooking Barcelona, because *Casa Battlo* had the flavor of pure fantasy.

O'Reilly took one last look at *Casa Battlo* then strolled to the foot of *La Rambla.* Standing beneath the statue of Columbus, he was pleased to see the *Adriatic Voyager,* sitting like a giant floating Las Vegas resort, at the Seven Seas terminal.

Chapter 5

It was only his second time on board a cruise ship. Ted Firestone had been the First Officer on a ship going to Hawaii and had gotten O'Reilly one of the unbooked rooms on a fall cruise. He had a general idea of how such a ship was laid out, but he was totally unfamiliar with any of the decks above those where passengers were allowed. Now he found himself on an elevator headed for the ship's bridge.

The elevator exited directly onto the bridge, where he was   greeted by a panoramic view of the harbor from 200 feet above the water. Ted Firestone, dressed in crisp white shirt and pants was sitting in a tall, well-cushioned, leather captain's chair next to two other similarly dressed men who were standing, the three of them engaged in conversation. In front of them was a Star Trek-worthy array of computer screens and toggle switches. At the sound of the elevator door, the Captain stopped talking and turned his head. A broad smile immediately creased his face.

"Welcome aboard!" Firestone greeted him, leaping out of his chair and striding across the shiny, planked floor to throw his arms around the taller O'Reilly.

"They really let you run this thing?" O'Reilly asked, disengaging himself and stepping back to take a longer look at his friend. Firestone was several inches shorter than he was and the shorter man had put on weight since he had last seen him and had grown a mustache. He beamed with the perpetual grin that O'Reilly remembered from the time they had been kids. It hadn't mattered what was going on—a reprimand from the principal or a huddle on the last play of the game to plan a hail-Mary pass to his favorite wide receiver—Ted Firestone was always grinning.

"It's not as fun as sailing our Lasers, but it's still a hoot, especially when we're on the high seas. And I don't capsize quite so often."

"Why the mustache? Do you have to look Italian to qualify for the job?"

Firestone grinned even wider. "Trust me, it helps. You should hear my Italian accent."

"I'll bring you a mandolin."

"How was Barcelona?"

"Like Olvera Street but with more bars." O'Reilly's face got serious. "Any new developments?"

Firestone pulled him to one side of the bridge in front of a wide computer screen that was dancing with incoming weather data. They were away from the other two crew members, who continued conversing with each other.

"Martini's security people are still scouring Naples," the Captain told him. "They figure that was where she was taken, although that doesn't mean she'd stay there. A lot of these human trafficking rings move their victims almost as soon as they grab them. But they're looking for leads. The head of the security team is still on the boat, talking to the crew. I've cancelled shore leaves until Magetti, that's the security chief, gets a chance to talk to all of them."

"Jesus, it's been almost a week. He's just now talking to the crew?"

"We needed to question the passengers first, since they were leaving the ship as soon as we reached Barcelona. She apparently liked hanging out in the crew's bar as much as with the other passengers. So now we have to talk anyone on the crew who spent time with her. This is our first chance."

"Speaking of bars, we're in port so you can drink, right?"

"As long as I'm not driving."

"Then get me settled in my room, and let's have a drink and you can fill me in completely."

Chapter 6

They met in the Officer's Bar, a dark, oak-paneled room with mahogany tables and heavy leather furniture strewn across a plush tan carpet, more like a private club than a ship's lounge, reminding O'Reilly of what the places to which he'd never been invited must look like. Firestone motioned him over to a circle of chairs in a dark corner of the room.

"Still drinking gin?" the captain asked.

"Until they invent something better."

Firestone raised a finger and a maroon-uniformed waiter appeared at his side. The man was skinny as a swizzle stick, balding, and probably in his late fifties, and Firestone addressed him as "Jerry" when he ordered a gin and tonic for O'Reilly and a whiskey and soda for himself. The man responded to the captain's order with a crisp, "yes, sir."

"The first thing to do is to get you caught up on what's been done so far," Firestone said. "I've asked Sergio Magetti to join us. He's Martini's head of security."

"How's he feel about you inviting me in?"

Firestone rolled his eyes. "He's pissed. Thinks it's an insult, an interference. He complained to Martini, but Mr. Martini told me to go ahead and do whatever I thought I needed to do, so to hell with Magetti's reaction." He flashed O'Reilly a confident grin.

33

It was nice to have his friend's backing but it wasn't an ideal situation. "I can't blame Magetti. I'd feel the same way," O'Reilly said.

"He's gonna blame you, I'm afraid. But he's a professional. He'll cooperate."

"That him?" O'Reilly was looking at a young man about thirty years old with a wide chest and a neck as thick as a pro football player's dressed in light gray slacks and a blue blazer. He had just entered the lounge and had fastened his eyes on the two of them.

"That's him," Firestone answered, standing and motioning for Magetti to join them.

The young man strode purposefully across the floor. He had a dark scowl on his handsome young face. His eyes were fastened on O'Reilly in a hard stare. He carried his arms stiffly at his sides, as if he was flexing his muscles beneath his jacket.

"Enter the Terminator," O'Reilly whispered.

Captain Firestone stuck out his hand, a gesture of friendliness but one that also served to stop Magetti in his beeline for O'Reilly.

"This is Brian O'Reilly. I invited him to help us find Julietta Martini. O'Reilly has a lot of experience finding people who are missing."

O'Reilly stood and stuck out his hand. He was several inches taller than Magetti, and his shoulders were even wider; but he was leaner and although more muscular, he lacked the Italian's bulk. Magetti shook his hand. His grip was strong, but not crushing. He was still glaring at O'Reilly.

"We've got the investigation under control," he said in heavily accented English. His expression was so pained that O'Reilly figured he must be suffering from constipation.

O'Reilly returned the young man's stare. "Sure you do. That's why the girl is still missing."

"Why don't we sit down," the Captain interjected as his two companions continued to stare each other down.

Everyone took his seat. Captain Firestone inquired if Magetti wanted a drink, but the security officer declined. "I've got work to do," Magetti said, dismissively.

"I'd like you to update Brian on what you've found out so far," Firestone said amicably. He was doing his best to ignore the Italian's animosity toward O'Reilly.

Magetti leaned back in his chair and heaved a resigned sigh. He had a broad, square face, smoothly shaven, with a wide, handsome mouth, presently pulled down at the corners in a sneer. His eyes were dark and brooding under thick, black eyebrows, and he stared straight across the table at O'Reilly. "I will update you, but I want it clear that I don't need your help, and I regard your being here as a waste of both your time and mine." He continued to glare at O'Reilly.

O'Reilly could think of dozens of things to say in response, but he didn't want to make things worse. "I' d probably feel the same way," he said, "if I was in the middle of an investigation and somebody I didn't know showed up to stick his nose into things. But Captain Firestone wants me to look into this, and your boss has agreed to it. Why don't we both just make the best of the situation?"

Magetti grunted an affirmation and the look on his face softened, if only a little. "As long as we both know that this isn't something I wanted or even welcome," he said. "I'll bring you up to date on what we've found out so far."

The waiter had returned to check on their drinks. Captain Firestone's glass was still half full, but O'Reilly had finished his gin and tonic and ordered another. The waiter turned stiffly toward Magetti. "And you, sir?"

The security officer relented and, without altering his dour demeanor, asked for a beer, then turned back toward O'Reilly. "Julietta was in her first year at the University of Florence," Magetti began, the scowl still on his face, just in case O'Reilly might forget that he was including the private detective in the investigation against his better judgment. "She communicated regularly with her parents, mostly her mother, and seemed to be doing fine. Last Tuesday she apparently boarded the *Adriatic Voyager,* when it docked in Livorno on the coast, using the name of Sylvia Marconi, a name she had been using at the University as part of our security measures to keep anyone from identifying her as Mr. Martini's daughter."

"Why take that precaution?" O'Reilly interrupted.

Magetti heaved a sigh. He pulled both of his arms back as if he were doing some kind of exercise to help his circulation or avoid a muscle cramp, although O'Reilly suspected it was more to show off his physique. "Mr. Martini is a wealthy man. He didn't want anyone deciding that they should try to do anything to his daughter in order to get to him. And Julietta agreed. She wanted to be treated as an ordinary student at the university, not as the daughter of a rich man."

O'Reilly wondered about the security man's use of his boss' daughter's first name, rather than something like "Miss Martini." After all, her father was his employer. Magetti's voice had softened when he talked about the girl. "How well did you know the girl?" O'Reilly interrupted him.

Magetti's face reddened. "I've known her since she was eleven years old. That was my first job with Mr. Martini... bodyguard protection for his wife and daughter.

"They needed a bodyguard?"

Magetti grimaced. "Mr. Martini does business with some not-so-nice people. That's why his daughter went under a different name at the university."

"It took me about five minutes on the internet to find out that she was a student at the university," O'Reilly said. "Not a very well-kept secret."

Magetti looked irritated. "She changed her name after she had already enrolled. That she was at the university was no secret—the papers already knew that—but her change of name kept it unclear to the majority of students who didn't know her face, which of their fellow students she actually was."

"And she had enough official papers—ID and passport—to board the ship under the assumed name?"

Magetti nodded. "We supplied all of those to her."

"So how did you know she was on the ship?"

"Her mother got worried because she hadn't heard from her. After a few days we made an inquiry to the National Police using her fake name, and their records showed her going through the customs checkpoint at Livorno and boarding the ship."

"When did you contact the ship?"

"Four days after the ship had left Livorno and had already stopped in Rome and Naples and was on its way to Venice we contacted Captain Firestone and asked him to locate Julietta—Sylvia, as she was listed as a passenger. She had a stateroom in her name, but no one could find her. Her room attendant said no one had been using the room since the ship had left Naples."

The new drinks had arrived, and O'Reilly took his gin and tonic and let it sit on the table. Magetti accepted his beer and immediately took a long drink from it, as if he'd stumbled upon a spring in the middle of the desert.

"What about her things—clothes, suitcase, bathroom items— were they still in her cabin or had she taken them?" O'Reilly asked.

Magetti put down his beer. He'd consumed a third of it. "Everything was still there. She hadn't packed up and left. She just hadn't come back to the ship."

O'Reilly turned to the Captain. "Do you keep track of who comes and goes?"

"Every passenger has an ID card that they slide through a machine as they leave and enter the ship. "

"And the ship left with a passenger still on shore?" O'Reilly asked.

"It happens. There are people who don't make it back to the ship. They go to the cruise line office and they get put on a plane or a bus and meet us at the next port."

"But she didn't do that."

Magetti answered. "She was never heard from again. The Captain found her on the list of passengers who had been left behind in Naples. But she hadn't contacted the cruise line office. That's when we knew she was gone."

"So tell me about your investigation," O'Reilly said, finally taking a sip of his second gin and tonic.

Magetti looked as if he was considering whether or not to answer. Then he nodded. "I put several staff ashore in Naples to start making inquiries, and I began interviewing passengers. Almost no one had even noticed her. She'd only been on the ship for three days, and it turned out that she had spent most of her time with the crew. She'd traveled on the *Adriatic Voyager* a few times before, with her father when she was a kid, and she knew a lot of the crew. She hung out with them in the crew bar or stayed in her cabin from what we can tell."

"Did she hang around with anyone special on the crew?"

Magetti nodded. "A young man—Serbian, name of Dmitri Dragic, although he was using a different name—not someone she apparently knew from before. He was on his first voyage as a crew member. He was a waiter. They spent a lot of time together. When she got off in Naples, he did too. He never returned either."

"So you think he took her?"

Magetti nodded; his expression had become morose. "That's our assumption. We checked on his background, got Interpol to run the prints taken from his room. He was using a fake name— Davidovic—but we got his real name through his prints. He has a record—assault, theft, pimping— arrests but no conviction, Serbia and Hungary."

"How do you know that Dragic isn't working for one of Martini's competitors? You said some of them were pretty rough characters."

'We don't for sure, but if this was something related to business, someone would have contacted Mr. Martini by now. We're pretty sure it's related to prostitution. That's in Dragic's background, and that's what happened to the other young women who were abducted from cruise ships."

"And whoever took her wouldn't know who she was? Who her father is?"

Magetti looked at him as if he were a kindergarten child who needed to have everything explained to him. "Human traffickers aren't mental giants. The *Camorra*, the local crime gangs, have joined up with Albanian and Serbian crime families to smuggle girls back and forth to Northern Europe. Those who grab the girls are just low level thugs like Dragic—low level but with some appeal to women—they drug the girls and move them out of the country as quickly as possible. With her fake ID there was no way a kidnapper would have known who she really was."

"And she wouldn't have told him?"

Magetti frowned. "She'd had it drilled into her that she was safer if no one knew who she was. My guess is that she thought it was wiser to not give away her identity."

O'Reilly was skeptical but decided to drop the subject. "So why are you still on the boat?" he asked. "Why don't you contact Interpol and get some help or at least the National police before this guy takes her out of Italy?"

Magetti's irritation was back... if it had ever left. "Right now I'm here because I was told that I needed to brief you. If we go to the police then it will be in the papers that Mr. Martini's daughter was kidnapped off of one of his own ships. He doesn't want that."

"You mean his business is more important to him than his daughter?"

Magetti stiffened. "Mr. Martini has faith in his own security services. We will find his daughter and bring her back safely."

"You've done this before—tracked a missing person?"

Magetti put down his beer and stared at him. "I'm Mr. Martini's head of security. He trusts me."

O'Reilly stared back. "You mean you'll keep this out of the press."

"I mean I'll find Julietta."

"She's liable to be pretty damaged goods by the time you do…" he looked Magetti directly in the eyes, "at the pace you're working."

Magetti bristled. He started to get up, looked as if he might come across the table at O'Reilly. Captain Firestone held out a hand, as if to restrain him. O'Reilly hadn't moved.

Magetti swallowed hard and settled back in his chair. "I don't need you're help or your opinions, Mr. O'Reilly."

"I guess not." O'Reilly took a sip from his drink. "Are you still interviewing the crew?"

"We're done. I've transferred most of my men back to Naples. I'm leaving this afternoon to head up the investigation there."

O'Reilly took another long sip. "Good for you. I'll stay on the ship for awhile. I want to talk to some of the crew before they get busy. Then I'll probably head for Naples and see what I can find."

Magetti frowned. "I don't want you tagging along with me. You'd just get in the way."

O'Reilly gave him an even look. "No I wouldn't, but I don't plan to follow you around anyway. I'll do my own investigating."

Magetti laughed. "You're not in the U.S. You don't know anything about Italy."

"I'm a quick study."

Magetti shook his head, then stood up to go. "I'll be collecting the rest of my staff, and we'll be leaving the ship. Thank you, Captain, for all of your help."

Captain Firestone stood up and shook the Italian's hand. O'Reilly nodded and Magetti shot him one last grimace, then turned and left.

"I see you haven't lost any of your social skills," Captain Firestone said as soon as Magetti was gone.

"This is cockeyed," O'Reilly answered. "I can't believe they wouldn't involve the police. What the hell is wrong with Martini? It's his daughter, for Christ sake."

"Martini's not your warmest person. He probably thinks his daughter is more expendable than his business."

"No wonder the girl ran away." He picked up his drink and took another long sip. "I'm not sure that her being missing isn't part of her just trying to get away from her parents. This whole kidnapping thing sounds fishy to me."

"Why? Human trafficking of girls and women for sex is big business in Europe. It involves hundreds of thousands of victims, mostly working for Eastern Europeans. It's not like the

U.S. where most of the prostitutes are either voluntary or are homeless kids. "

"But who picks the daughter of one of the richest men in Europe? If she was kidnapped her captors would make a lot more money asking her father for ransom than selling her as just another sex slave."

Firestone shrugged, as if what O'Reilly had said might or might not be true. "Either way, her father wants her back… and without headlines."

O'Reilly gulped the last of his drink the stood up. "Then I guess I'd better get busy."

Chapter 7

Captain Firestone had turned O'Reilly over to Gioppe Bruno, the ship's Chief of Security. As he gave the LA detective a tour of the 14-story behemoth that was the *Adriatic Voyager*, Bruno launched into a diatribe against the owner's security têam, Sergio Magetti, in particular.

"He treated us as if we were some local *polizia* and they were the *Carabinieri*. The cretin actually said to me, 'go back to making sure no one crowds in line in the buffet.' " Bruno looked as if he wanted to spit out something that tasted bad. He was a small man, dapper despite the same white uniform that all the officers on the ship wore. He had a small, rat-like face, a pencil-thin mustache and black hair combed neatly back and graying at the temples. He walked with a mincing step that fit with his title of *Chief of Security* about as well as "Hooray for Hollywood" would fit as a fight song for the L.A. Kings hockey team. O'Reilly noticed that his fingernails were manicured.

They had descended to the third deck, just at the level of the dock, where tons of food and other supplies were being loaded onto the ship. The *Adriatic Voyager* carried two thousand passengers and a thousand crew members, so the amount of supplies that was required was enormous. In front of them two female and one male crew members dragged and pushed a narrow dolly loaded five feet high with boxes of toilet tissue down a corridor.

45

"So how'd they know who to interview?" O'Reilly asked.

"They began asking questions… not too aggressively, either," Bruno answered. "They said they didn't want to alarm any passengers or raise any suspicions about the girl being missing."

"But the crew must have known, didn't they?"

"That kind of thing gets around a ship as fast as an outbreak of *norovirus*. But as soon as Magetti found out about Davidovic—or I guess it turns out his name was Dragic—he wasn't interested in anything else. He was sure that the girl had been kidnapped and he thought he knew who did it."

"He didn't talk to other crew members?"

"One or two, but not many."

"I thought that was why he stayed on the ship instead of going to Naples with the rest of his men."

"He was only on board so he could talk to you. The rest of his men were in Naples."

O'Reilly shook his head. "I guess he thought he had his man in Dragic." He reminded himself that Magetti had mostly been a bodyguard, not an investigator.

"Probably so," Bruno answered. "But the Martini girl had other friends among the crew."

"Friends Magetti didn't interview?"

"Several."

"I'd like to talk to them, them… and also the crew members that Magetti *did* interview."

46

Bruno's description of the investigation that had been conducted on board the ship hadn't given him confidence in the findings so far.

The crew was getting ready for the impending onslaught of passengers, and most of the people Bruno was able to find were rushing around getting everything in place for the two-thousand new guests who would come aboard, feeling as hungry and thirsty as clients leaving a Weight Watchers summer camp. The only times to talk to crew members were sometime after midnight when the dining rooms were closed and most of the passengers had retired or right now, before any passengers had come aboard. What now appeared to be frenetic crew activity, would appear calm compared to the rest of the cruise when everyone was busy serving the ship's perpetually demanding guests in one way or another. Bruno gave him a security card that, he assured him, "will give you access to any place you want to go on the ship."

APPOINTMENT IN MYKONOS

Chapter 8

O'Reilly began with Anka Sokolov, a
striking chestnut-haired Bulgarian girl who was
Maître d' in one of the ship's fancier dining
rooms—one where guests had to pay an extra cover
charge for the privilege of dining. *Provence*, the
French restaurant where she worked, was an
impressive room, and the waiters and waitresses
were in the middle of setting tables, which were
covered in white linen tablecloths and were
surrounded by high-backed cushioned chairs. The
restaurant was on the 12th deck of the ship and had
large windows, decorated with arched white
latticework, looking out over the ocean—or right
now over the harbor. The décor was French, in
keeping with the theme of the restaurant. The walls
were covered in red damask wallpaper, and the table
lamps had soft lighting and crimson fringe hanging
from their shades. It reminded O'Reilly of a French
whorehouse. Not that he'd ever been to a French
whorehouse... except in his dreams.

When they located Anka she was directing
the set up in the dining room, but a word from
Bruno convinced her to turn over her duties to an
assistant and talk to O'Reilly.

"You look too young to be a Maître d',"
O'Reilly said. She had an oval face surrounded by
dark hair, which framed her milky-white features in
long silky waves, reaching to her shoulders. Her
mouth was broad and curved in a perpetual smile,

48

with full lips, which she had colored a pale peach. Her eyes were large and almond-shaped with long, black lashes that contrasted with her deep green irises. They had retired to one of the ship's lounges, *Joie de Vivre*, which had an art deco theme with garish pink and blue rugs and lots of chrome. The bar specialized in champagne and served caviar and foie gras to the pampered passengers of the line. "I'm surprised that they have female Maître d's on an Italian cruise line," he added.

"The company recognizes ability. And I know how to sell myself." She smiled a confident smile, cheerful, but self-possessed enough to carry the message that she wasn't *just* a pretty face, although a pretty face she certainly was.

"I'm sold," O'Reilly replied, letting his eyes drift across the gentle curves of her body then making eye contact as he smiled at her in appreciation. "You sound like someone who knows what you want."

"And I'm not afraid to go after it… in a nice way, of course," she flashed a broad smile that showed off her white, even teeth. "Things go easier when others want you to succeed. And they have to like you for that to happen."

"You're easy to like." Was he flirting with her? He guessed he was flattering himself by thinking that she might be flirting with him. After all, he was more than one and half times her age.

She was sitting on a short divan wearing a crisp white ship's uniform, much like those of ship's officers, except that it included a skirt instead of pants. She wore a short-sleeved blouse, which was cut low enough to reveal a generous cleavage, which she was making no effort to conceal. She sat with her legs crossed, which was proper and demure, but accentuated the curve of her thighs and buttocks. She wasn't a slim girl and her voluptuous body nicely rounded out the tight uniform. She had a habit of finishing every sentence with a bright smile, which showed her white teeth and a pair of dimples in each cheek.

"I'm glad you like me," she said, still smiling. "You don't have to, you know. Mr. Bruno said you are a friend of the Captain. And you've been hired by Mr. Martini himself. That means I'll be nice to you." As if to emphasize her words, she gave his broad shoulders an appreciative look.

"I'd like you to like me too," he answered, smiling back at her. "I'm kind of a sweet guy myself."

Her smile widened. "I was pretty sure you were." She lowered her eyelids seductively. Then she looked up. "But I'd better start answering your questions, because I have to get back to the dining room to supervise my staff."

She was right. He needed to find out what this young woman knew about Julietta Martini. "You met Julietta Martini when she was eating in your dining room?"

"I recognized her as soon as she sat down in the restaurant on her first night aboard," Anka recalled. "I'd heard that Mr. Martini had a daughter not much younger than me, so I'd looked her up once on the internet and saw her picture. She's very beautiful, you know."

He didn't know and her question reminded him that he needed to get a picture of Julietta before he went ashore looking for her. "She ate alone?"

"Always." She smiled shyly. "She didn't socialize much with the other passengers. She didn't even go ashore when we stopped in Rome."

Anka was beautiful herself, and O'Reilly couldn't help but let his gaze wander up and down her body as she sat and talked to him. He was captivated by her smile and figured that the perky personality was something she'd developed in her work with the restaurant's customers. She probably regarded O'Reilly in the same category as her senior citizen cruise ship passengers.

He reluctantly shifted his gaze from her body before she accused him of being a dirty old man. He focused on her dark green eyes while he resisted popping the cork on one of the many bottles of champagne on display. "So when you recognized her, did you say anything to her?"

"Not at first. When she gave me her room number to cover her bill I saw that it was listed under another name, so I thought I might be mistaken. I said something to one of my waiters about her looking like the owner's daughter and he took a closer look. He's an older man who's been with the ship a lot of years. He came back and told me that it was Julietta, Mr. Martini's daughter. He recognized her from when she had been on the ship with her father. Then he went up and said hello to her. She seemed happy to see him."

"Not upset that she'd been recognized?"

"Not at all."

"So how did *you* get to know her?"

"After Melchior, that's the waiter, talked to her, I introduced myself and told her how honored I felt serving the owner's daughter."

"What did she say?"

"She said she didn't want any of the passengers to find out who she was, but she knew she'd be recognized by some of the crew. Then she asked me if she could hang out with me in the crew's bar after I finished my shift."

"And did she?"

Anka smiled brightly, her white teeth showing in a broad smile that brought back her dimples. "Yeah. Right away that first night. As soon as she came into the bar a couple of other older crew came by and said hello to her because they recognized her. In fact, she became sort of a main attraction among the crew because of who she was."

"So she used her own name with the crew?"

Her face became more serious. "She told us she was taking a 'vacation' from school and from her family and she didn't want her family to know she was on the ship. We all agreed to keep her secret... like a mystery." She looked as if she might be ready to giggle.

It never hurt to get a pretty girl giggling. "I'm glad to hear you can keep secrets."

She smiled slyly. "Oh I can keep lots of secrets."

He almost giggled himself.

"So how much did you see her after that?" It was time to get back to his questions.

She resumed her serious manner, but her eyes still shone brightly. "She was only on board for two more nights and for the day when we were in port in *Civitavecchia*, near Rome. But I saw her both nights at dinner and then later in the crew's bar. The rest of the time I don't know what she did, except I know that when we were in port, she still came to the crew's bar because the crew have more time to hang out when most of the passengers are off the ship sightseeing. She said that she had no interest in going ashore in Rome because she'd visited it so many times before."

He made a mental note of her comment. It didn't fit with Julietta leaving the ship in Naples. "Did she say what she planned to do when the cruise was over?"

"She had a ticket for the return trip as far as Livorno. That's what she said, anyway. She was just trying to get away for a few days."

"Did she say why?"

The young woman looked thoughtful. "Not really. I think she felt bad about worrying her mother, but she didn't feel bad about her father. She looked angry every time anyone mentioned him."

"Did she talk about him?"

She shrugged her shoulders. "I remember once when someone asked her how her father liked owning a cruise line, she said, 'ask his business partners, I don't know how my father feels about anything.' Another time someone brought up the basketball team her father owned and she said something like, 'he gets to adopt a bunch of sons instead of the daughter he never wanted.'"

"That's pretty bitter stuff."

"Everybody on the crew who's met her father say he's kind of an asshole." She looked suddenly fearful. "You're not going to tell anyone I said that are you?"

"I can keep secrets too," he said, winking.

A look of relief passed across her face. She smiled broadly, showing off her teeth and bringing back her dimples.

"Who else did she make friends with among the crew?" he asked.

"Dmitri. Did the other security guy tell you about him?"

"He mentioned him. Tell me about him."

She shifted her rounded hips on the divan. For the first time since their conversation had begun she looked uncomfortable, knitting her pencil-thin eyebrows as if contemplating things she'd rather not say. "Nobody really knew the guy. This was his first trip on the *Voyager*. To tell you the truth, most of the crew thought he was kind of a jerk. He was always late for his shift and a lot of the time he seemed drunk. And he was constantly hitting on the female crew members."

"But he and Julietta were friends?"

She cocked her head to one side as if she were thinking. "I'm not sure I'd say they were friends. He hung around her a lot. I think he was attracted to the fact that she was rich."

"What makes you say that?"

"He asked me a lot about her—because she and I had become friends. He wanted to know how much her father was worth, whether she had her own house, a car, things like that. He asked me to ask her if she bought a lot of expensive jewelry."

"What did you tell him?"

"To fuck off and mind his own business." Her face colored, as if she was embarrassed using such language. Probably because she was talking to an "older" man, O'Reilly thought.

He'd been operating on the assumption that whoever had kidnapped Julietta hadn't known who she was. That was the only explanation of why anyone who was trafficking in young women would abduct someone rich and famous. But Dragic had known full well who she was—he was even more interested in her because of that. Things were becoming more and more mysterious.

"So how did Miss Martini feel about Dmitri?"

"She thought he was a creep. But she was nice to him. She was nice to everybody," Anka said, with a bright smile of her own. Her eyes shone brightly when she smiled.

"I understood that she spent a lot of time with him."

"She was only on board for three days. But he spent a lot of time around her—as much as he could. But trust me, she wasn't what you would call *with* him. She just couldn't get rid of him."

"But I heard they left the ship together in Naples."

"Really?" She raised one shapely eyebrow as if she was skeptical. "I know she got bored and decided to go ashore. Maybe she knew some people in Naples. But they didn't go ashore together. I'm sure of it. He was the last person she'd go ashore with."

"But he left the ship in Naples."

She nodded. "Jumped ship. I heard he had a six months contract with the ship, but he left in the middle of his first cruise. I guess he got bored. And he wasn't making much progress hitting on women."

"There were other women besides Julietta?"

"He made a pass at everyone. Even me."

"I can hardly blame him," O'Reilly said, throwing in another wink for good measure. "But I'm sure you didn't fall for it."

"I'm very selective about who I go out with," she said, winking back at him.

He tried to keep his spirits in rein. She was probably just humoring an old man. "Anybody else fall for it? Someone less selective than you?"

"We had only been a sea for a week or so before Naples. We left from Malaga, then picked up new passengers in Barcelona; we stopped in Toulon, then Livorno, where Julietta joined us, then to Rome, then Naples where he jumped ship. But he made the most of his time on board. He tried to bed everyone he could—without any luck. Everyone knew he was a scumbag." She paused, thinking again. "Except Marina. Marina would have been a sucker for anyone. She was very naïve, even though she was quite pretty in her own way."

"Was?"

"She was only going as far as Naples. She'd been with the ship for almost a year and her contract was up. She left in Naples."

Magetti had never mentioned another crew member leaving the ship. Maybe because her leaving had been scheduled, since her contract was up, unlike Dragic, who had walked off in the middle of his job. He wondered if Magetti even knew about Marina. The more he learned, the shoddier the security man's investigation appeared.

"What was Marina's full name?"

"Stepovich, she was Polish."

He wrote the name on his notepad. "But you said she got off in Naples. Did she live there or in Poland?"

"Naples. She lived with her parents in Naples. There's a large Polish community within the city."

Something else he didn't know. "Tell me about Marina and Dmitri."

"She was a sweet girl. But she was so shy that she never came to the crew parties or anything like that. She sort of left herself out of everything. She didn't drink, and that's a big minus if you're part of the crew. A lot of them get drunk almost every night."

"But she and Dmitri became a couple?"

She nodded. Her perky smile had returned. "It was kinda weird. He zeroed in on her almost from the start, right after he got on the ship, even though he made passes at other girls at the same time. He spent as much time with Marina as he did hanging around Julietta. She was really smitten by him. He was a good talker, especially if you were naïve and didn't know that he was talking bullshit." Her face colored again.

"It's OK to swear around an older gentleman," O'Reilly said.

She looked his long frame up and down, her gaze finally coming to rest on his face. "You're not old. We're not allowed to swear around passengers is all. Sometimes I forget myself."

"Go ahead and forget yourself. I'm not a real passenger." He flashed her his most winning smile. Now that she'd told him that she didn't think he was old, he took another quick survey of her figure. His assessment made it even more difficult for him to refocus on their conversation.

"So she really fell for him?" he asked.

"Absolutely. I tried to tell her that he was a jerk, but she wouldn't listen. Not to me or to anyone else. She didn't even notice him hitting on other women."

So Dragic had found himself another victim besides Julietta Martini. Sergio Magetti might be barking up the completely wrong tree. Or maybe not. Julietta was missing and Dragic still appeared to be the best lead. He needed to track down Marina Stepovich in Naples and find out if she was also missing.

He'd get off the ship tomorrow and go to Naples himself and look for both Julietta and Marina. But that was tomorrow.

Anka was looking antsy. "They're going to board the passengers in a little while. I have to get back to work. My dining room is the pride of the ship, and I work hard to keep it that way. You should visit us for dinner."

"I'd love to but I probably won't have time. But that doesn't mean I won't see you. I'll need to talk to some more crew members tonight. Do you think you could introduce me to those who spent time with Julietta?"

"I'm working pretty late."

"But you'll be in the crew's bar after work."

She nodded, her smile becoming a little more fetching than before. Or maybe O'Reilly was just imagining that. "You want to join me there?"

"I've been told that's the best time to talk to crew members." He flashed a fetching smile of his own. "Besides I need to buy you a drink for spending all this time with me."

"It's been a pleasure," she said, smiling back.

"Yes it has."

They both rose and she gave him a brief hug. Not so brief that he didn't notice the soft pressure of her substantial breasts against his chest. "See you about midnight," she said.

He could hardly wait.

Chapter 9

The ship had begun to move. O'Reilly peered out of the small round porthole that was his cabin's window, as the pink, white and gray buildings lining Barcelona's harbor appeared and then disappeared, at first slowly, then gaining speed, as the ship pulled out to sea.

He'd gone through the ship's safety drill— held in the casino—learning where the passengers from his deck were supposed to "muster" in case of an emergency and how to put on his lifejacket. His fellow passengers appeared to be a mix of older and younger couples, the older ones sometimes so geriatric that had they not traveled in couples, able to help each other by mutual leaning and hand-holding, he doubted that they would have been able to move from one place on the boat to another. There was also a large number of singles—mostly young, but some closer to his age—more females than males and usually in groups of two or three, although he noticed one or two passengers who appeared to be traveling alone. It made him think that a cruise ship wasn't really such great a place to look for a victim if you wanted to kidnap someone. But he remembered Melissa Kramer, who'd been abducted in Puerto Vallarta during a shore excursion and the six other young females that Ted Firestone had told him had gone missing in Europe already in this cruise season. Maybe it was just a matter of separating the prospective abductee from her friends.

And Julietta Martini had been traveling alone.

He looked around at his room. It was considerably larger than the cabin on his sailboat, with two twin beds, a nightstand and a chair, built-in drawers and a bathroom and shower that put his boat's head to shame. He was used to living in small quarters, but he was also bored. He was eager to resume questioning the crew and particularly to have that promised drink with Anka Sokolov, although he'd probably gotten all the information about Julietta Martini from the young woman that she possessed. But he liked the idea of talking to her again… and of spending more time ogling that amazing figure of hers. Or whatever else he might be able to do with it.

And he was thirsty. It was time to venture out of his cabin and sample one of the ship's bars.

He walked along the brightly colored carpet in the passageway, which featured paintings of starfish and seashells on the walls, to the middle of the ship where the stairs and elevators were positioned. He felt as if he was walking along the corridor of a hotel rather than a ship. But cruise ships were basically floating hotels—hotels and shopping malls—complete with their half dozen or so restaurants, their boutique shops and their swimming pools, shuffleboard courts and exercise rooms.

APPOINTMENT IN MYKONOS

When he reached his deck's common area he found three twenty-something women standing in front of the elevator wearing the skimpiest bikinis he'd ever seen, towels draped over their shoulders and tubes of suntan lotion in their hands. They were talking excitedly in English about getting the last rays of the day's sun and of what kind of drinks they were going to consume when they reached the pool area, which was on the 12th deck. He immediately made a decision to go to one of the bars on the 12th deck. When the elevator arrived he held the door for them to enter and smiled his most captivating smile.

They all giggled.

"Need any help applying that suntan lotion?" He asked.

They all giggled again.

"You're welcome to join us, but you'll have to ditch the suit first," one of the girls said, eyeing his seersucker sport coat, his suntan pants and his open-necked blue Oxford cloth shirt. She was a black haired, dark-skinned beauty, with wide, almond-shaped brown eyes who appeared to be nearly O'Reilly's height, until he looked down and saw that she was wearing six-inch heels with her bikini. She obviously wasn't going on deck to swim.

"I tried to change into my swimming trunks but I was all thumbs," he answered. "Maybe if you could come to my cabin and give me a hand…?"

"Very funny. Trash the suit and you're welcome to join us for a drink," she answered, giving an approving look at his broad shoulders.

"Maybe later."

Her invitation was tempting but he knew he'd feel more comfortable in the dark confines of a bar than lying on a deck chair listening to the chatter of three young females, no matter how attractive they might be. On the other hand, maybe after a few drinks he'd feel differently. He often felt differently about things after a few drinks.

He and the girls arrived at the 12th deck and he reluctantly watched them leave for the pool area. The dark-skinned one in the heels walked like a model on a catwalk, her long hips swaying gracefully as she placed one six-inch heeled shoe in front of the other. She looked back over her head and gave him one last smile.

He smiled back. Then he began to wonder if he really was getting old. Five years ago he would have made a beeline for his cabin to change into a pair of bathing trunks. Now he was headed for the bar and solitude.

He walked through the buffet area, where at least half of the passengers seemed to have already settled-in to taste the non-stop food that characterized a cruise ship, and he finally found the English-style pub. There were three lone male drinkers at the bar and a young couple in swim outfits at one of the tables near the entrance.

He took a place at the bar but well away from any of the other male drinkers. He ordered a gin and tonic from the bartender, a short, round man in his mid-thirties with balding black hair and friendly dark eyes who wore one of the ship's signature maroon uniforms that all the crew who weren't officers or weren't costumed for one of the extra-charge restaurants wore.

His eyes were drawn to a couple, passing in front of the pub's entrance. The woman, who was middle-aged with a slim figure and very large breasts and was dressed in a pair of pink shorts and a white blouse, was frighteningly familiar. She was searching the bar as if deciding whether the couple should enter or not. When her eyes fastened on O'Reilly, they went wide in shock.

He nodded his head in her direction—a sign that he recognized his ex-wife. He recognized her companion also, even though the man hadn't noticed him yet. The man, who was nearly as tall as O'Reilly, was dressed in long slacks, sandals and a loose-fitting Hawaiian shirt, which hung like the skirts of a Bedouin tent over his sizeable belly. He was turning his red, round, heavily-jowled face to the woman to see what had caused her to jump. Her gaze was still directed toward O'Reilly and following her line of sight, the man put his hands on his hips in a gesture of disgust. The woman dragged him toward O'Reilly.

"Jesus Christ, Brian, what in the hell are you doing here? This is too much of a coincidence." The woman was smiling, and she held out her arms as if expecting a hug.

"Too much is right," her companion said, a massive scowl clouding his face. "He's going to ruin our vacation."

O'Reilly was still in shock, although he was trying his best to conceal it. He put an arm out and, in response to her warm clasp of him against her ample chest, offered a minimalist hug, not rising from his bar stool. "This is weird, Phyllis," he told his ex-wife. "I haven't seen you in three years and we live in the same city. Now I come to Europe and here you are." He was ignoring the other man's presence.

"Bullshit," the other man interrupted, his voice a low growl. "You found out we were going on this cruise and you decided to take the same trip so you could screw things up for us." He leaned toward O'Reilly, his scowl still in place on his fleshy face and his big, meaty hands clenched in fists, as if he was preparing himself for a fight.

"I wouldn't get on the same ship with you on purpose for all the castanets in Spain," he replied to his old nemesis, Derrick Sterling of the LAPD. "I didn't even know you two were dating." He looked over at his ex-wife and started to smile. "Or have you gotten married? It would be a match made in heaven… or someplace."

"It's none of your fucking business," Sterling answered. He moved threateningly toward O'Reilly, who still hadn't gotten up off his stool.

"Easy, Derrick," O'Reilly said, a smile pirouetting around the corners of his mouth. "You don't want me to knock you on your butt right here in front of all of these passengers, do you? You didn't like it last time I did that, although the guys in the station got a big kick out of it, as I recall."

The heavy-set detective's face blanched with fear, then turned red and angry. "Did you hear that, Phyllis, he threatened me?" He turned to the bartender, who was standing about two yards away. "This passenger just threatened me. Call your ship's security!"

The bartender's eyes widened. He backed away, unsure what to do. "Calm down please," he finally managed to sputter.

O'Reilly was still smiling. "I'm not sure you want to call security, Derrick. I'm working for them. I'm an employee of the cruise line. I could get you thrown off the ship."

"What?" Phyllis asked. She hadn't seemed particularly bothered by the confrontation between her companion and he ex-husband; in fact, she seemed to have enjoyed it. But she was plainly surprised by O'Reilly's claim that he was working for the cruise line.

"That's bullshit!" Sterling growled. "What do you mean you're working for the cruise line?"

"Yes, Brian," his wife echoed. "What do you mean?"

"Ted Firestone—you remember him, Phyllis—my friend? He's the captain of this ship. He hired me on a case. I'm in the middle of an investigation." He turned toward Sterling. "You might be interfering with my investigation. Maybe I should call security."

"You're an asshole, O'Reilly." Sterling turned toward Phyllis. "We're getting off this tub at the first port. I'm not taking any cruise that this shmuck is on."

For the first time Phyllis looked alarmed. "No! We can't. I've waited for this for months. I'm not going to give it up just because Brian is here. We'll just avoid him. I know we can do that."

O'Reilly stared at her. For all the animosity he'd felt over the years toward her, he didn't really want to hurt her. "You don't have to get off the boat tomorrow. I'm leaving the cruise at Toulon. I'm only on for tonight. My work's taking me ashore."

"Good riddance," Sterling said.

"Oh thank you," Phyllis said. She reached out and gave O'Reilly another hug.

This time O'Reilly gave her a nice long hug, then a slow kiss on the mouth.

Sterling started toward him.

O'Reilly disengaged himself from his ex-wife. He held up a hand toward Sterling. "Ah, ah, Lieutenant. That was just for old time's sake. Now don't make me do something to you for old time's sake."

Sterling backed away. His eyes were bulging as he stared at O'Reilly in anger. Then he turned to Phyllis and grabbed her by the hand. "C'mon. We're leaving." He dragged her back out of the bar. As they left she looked back at O'Reilly and gave him a smile.

He blew her a kiss.

APPOINTMENT IN MYKONOS

Chapter 10

Two gin and tonics, a bowlful of peanuts and an hour of thinking hadn't gotten him any more than a piece of peanut stuck between two of his back teeth. He dug the fragment out with a toothpick and paid for the drinks with the on-ship credit card, which Captain Firestone had provided him. He was to have dinner at the Captain's table in the ship's main dining room, but that wasn't for another two hours. He debated donning his swimming trunks and heading for the pool to see if the three young women from the elevator might still be there. But the sun was already setting and he didn't' relish parading around in swimming trunks in the cool Mediterranean evening air.

Instead he descended to deck seven and the casino.

The casino on the *Adriatic Voyager* would have fit nicely into one of the washrooms at *Caesar's* or the *Bellagio*. There were a couple hundred slot machines, four poker tables, four blackjack tables, two roulette wheels and a craps table… and a bar. The staff were dressed in maroon pants and white shirts and ties while the female staff wore skimpy waitress outfits that showed off their breasts and legs. The passenger were mostly wearing shorts and flip flops.

The Blackjack table in the *Adriatic Voyager's* casino fronted a low-stakes game, which was right up O'Reilly's alley. He was a better than average player but gambling was the one area of his life, with the exception of swimming in the cold night air, where he avoided risks. He never bet more than he could afford to lose.

Most of the players at his table appeared to be harried husbands whose wives were having their hair done or were sunning themselves by the pool, their spouses playing cards just for something to do while they consumed the alcohol that showed up at their shoulder on the tray of a well-endowed young waitress about every five minutes. It was a pastime that made sense to O'Reilly.

After about half an hour he'd won forty dollars and it was time to quit while he was ahead. He strolled over to the bar and ordered his third gin of the evening. This time he avoided the peanuts.

"Pretty tame action," the man dressed in neatly pressed slacks and an open-necked silk shirt who was sitting on the stool to his left, said.

"I guess it's something to do when the sun goes down and you're not ready to go to dinner," O'Reilly answered. The thought of dinner reminded him that he was getting hungry.

'There are some serious gamblers on board," the man continued. He was only partially turned to O'Reilly, and his face wasn't fully visible. What could be seen of it looked like a thirtyish, clean-shaven young man, the kind who might sell stocks or life insurance on the mainland.

O'Reilly hoped he wasn't in for a sales pitch from someone who refused to accept the idea that he was on vacation. He nodded and continued to sip his drink.

"I'm not talking about in here," the man added.

"Do tell," O'Reilly said, his gaze fixed on the bottles behind the bar.

"There's another room just beyond that corridor over there. It's smaller, but they've got a roulette wheel and two or three card games. You can only get in by special invitation."

O'Reilly was becoming mildly interested. Not that he wanted to join any high stakes game, but the presence of such a room on a family–oriented cruise ship seemed odd. And he was usually interested in life's oddities, especially if they might be related to his job.

"You've been in there?" He asked, turning to get a better look at his informant. The man, a pudgy young fellow in his early thirties with short, neatly combed hair and wearing a pair of dark slacks and a silk Hawaiian shirt, really did look like a fresh-faced salesman, gone a little fat—probably as a result of success. He appeared to be one of those people who just liked to talk.

"I'm here with some business friends. Supposedly we're here to gamble. The play's too rich for me. I watched for awhile, but then I got thirsty and came out here."

"They don't have a bar?"

"Just waiters who wander the floor. They were too slow for my taste." As if to make his point he held up his empty glass for to the bartender to bring him another. He was drinking scotch on ice.

O'Reilly finished his drink. "Thanks," he told the man. "Maybe I'll take a quick look myself."

"You need to be invited."

He thought about the security card Bruno had given him. "I have been."

APPOINTMENT IN MYKONOS

Chapter 11

The room was exactly as the stranger at the bar had described: its presence concealed behind a nondescript door off the corridor, marked only by a sign that said "Private." A burly attendant at the door blocked his way as soon as he stepped through the door, but when he showed him his security card, the man stepped aside and seemed to lose all interest in him. A waiter in a far corner seemed even less interested in his presence than the man at the door had been, which was too bad because O'Reilly was thirsty.

The majority of the customers were men and fewer than half of them were wearing the shorts and Hawaiian shirts which seemed to be the official uniform of most of the ship's passengers. The rest were dressed like the man at the bar: in slacks, street shoes and sport shirts; several of them wore jackets, as did O'Reilly. A couple of men were wearing tuxedos, and there were a few women in the room, wearing long dresses and hanging on older men's arms. Instead of the red, white, blue and yellow plastic chips that were being used in the main casino, players at each of the three tables were using shiny metal rectangular gaming plaques, their denominations, in multiples of a thousand dollars stamped on their fronts. The games in this room were definitely different.

He cruised the room, taking in the play at each table with no intention of joining in himself.

Although he suspected he would be able to hold his own, he couldn't afford the stakes in a room like this. And anyway, he was an employee of the cruise line. His security card had proved it.

The hushed mood of the room echoed the grim faces of each of the players at the three poker tables. O'Reilly noticed that one game was already deep into bets of over ten thousand dollars a hand. The only frivolity was at the roulette wheel where a small crowd had gathered to watch the action. O'Reilly chased the drinks waiter around the room until he caught him and put in an order for a gin and tonic, then sauntered over to the fun and games at the colorful wheel in the corner.

An elderly man, with a face that sported more wrinkles than a month-old orange, was leaning heavily against the felt-covered table in front of the wheel. He looked as if he might need to request oxygen at any moment… if he could find a waiter to bring him some. A jet-black hairpiece clung precariously to his scalp. His liver-spotted hands danced with a Parkinsonian tune across his pile of ten-thousand-dollar plaques, while his eyes swept the table to assess the inclinations of the other four men who were playing the wheel. He wasn't saying anything but his mouth moved in a palsied chewing motion. Unlike the other well-dressed customers in the room, he was dressed in a light-blue warm-up outfit that hung on his skeletal frame like the complimentary bathrobe hung on the hanger in O'Reilly's closet. In front of him was a pile of thousand-dollar roulette chips and with jerky deliberation he pushed a pile of five of them onto the black seventeen. The crowd clapped and the old man pumped a shaky fist in the air as if his bet had already won.

Standing next to the elderly gentleman was a younger man, with unruly brown hair that looked as if it had been ruffled by the wind on one of the outside decks. He was dressed in a white linen suit that made him look like he'd taken the Bogart role in Casablanca too seriously. He stared with earnest deliberation marking his ruddy face then placed a one-hundred dollar chip between a pair of numbers, repeated his bet on another pair and then, for safety's sake, put another two-hundred dollars on the outside red. The group around the table clapped politely.

Two more players, both fat men in shorts, one sporting a gaudy orange Hawaiian shirt and the other a turquoise short-sleeved polo shirt, placed one-hundred dollar chips on about five numbers each. Both of them turned to the crowd for applause, and were rewarded with a gracious ripple.

The only other player was a tall, thin man in a black tuxedo. In his early thirties, he had the aura of an aristocrat. With his drooping mustache and heavily lidded eyes he surveyed the bets of his three fellow players and frowned. In front of him was a small pile of one-thousand dollar roulette chips. He casually distributed about three or four of the chips across several numbers. He didn't glance at the crowd and it answered him with wary silence.

APPOINTMENT IN MYKONOS

The croupier spun the wheel and everyone's eyes were glued to the ball as it swirled around the wheel, then started clattering toward the numbers. The crowd began whooping with excitement, and the bouncing sphere appeared ready to fall on the black seventeen. The aristocratic man in the tuxedo pointed toward the ball and let out a loud exclamation at the same time as the white-clad young man fumed and pounded the table so hard that he knocked over his drink, causing a momentary uproar in the cluster of people around him. As the ball edged toward number seventeen, O'Reilly watched the man in the tuxedo nudge one of his thousand dollar chips onto the red twenty-five, just before the ball slid past seventeen and came to rest on his number.

A shout of triumph went up from the small crowd around the table. The man in the tuxedo gave a small bow and patiently waited for the croupier to reimburse his table chips with house plaques, at the rate of thirty-five to one for his thousand dollar bet.

It wasn't the most skillful instance of *past posting* O'Reilly had witnessed, but it wasn't bad. If he hadn't had a case in which he'd had to follow a casino cheat in Las Vegas and Reno, he wouldn't have been able to pick up the play. He was pretty sure that it was a cooperative effort between the young man in white, who had spilled his drink to distract both the crowd and the croupier, and the man in the tuxedo. The croupier looked momentarily confused, since with the small number of bets, he'd probably memorized where they were, but then he shot a glance toward a swarthy man in a white evening jacket who stood near one of the poker tables, and the man gave him a nod, which seemed to take care of the croupier's misgivings, and he paid the tuxedoed man his winnings.

O'Reilly watched as the young man in the tuxedo haughtily accepted the congratulations from the appreciative onlookers and made his way to the door of the gaming room and no doubt straight to the cashier in the main casino. The young man in the white suit remained behind and placed a one hundred dollar bet on another number. O'Reilly knew that he would keep playing—and probably losing—for another half hour at least, before leaving the casino and meeting up with his partner to split the winnings. After a thirty-five thousand dollar win, neither of the men would be back. He wouldn't be surprised if they left the ship at the first stop.

"You just got taken by the guy who walked out that door," O'Reilly said quietly. He was standing next to the man in the dinner jacket who had given the croupier the nod for the payout and who had given him a mildly interested look when he'd sidled up next to him, but now seemed more captivated by the poker game in front of him.

"You some kind of policeman?" the man asked, turning his head to look O'Reilly over. "We're in international waters. You don't have any jurisdiction." The man had a dark, round face with one of those five-o'clock shadows that never seemed to be completely removed. He had thick black eyebrows and slicked back dark hair that almost glistened with oil. He was thick bodied and barrel chested, but with the dinner jacket, it wasn't clear if he was mostly muscle or fat. He stared at O'Reilly with a flat, almost bored expression.

"I'm on your side," O'Reilly answered. "Martini hired me to find something he lost."

The man's eyes flickered with sudden interest. "You're the American dick that the captain brought on board."

O'Reilly smiled at the man's use of a pulp fiction expression for "private detective." "That's right. So you don't care if someone cheats your casino out of several thousand dollars?"

"I didn't say I didn't care. We don't usually like to have anything ugly happen in front of our passengers."

"You mean something ugly is going to happen to the guy in the tuxedo?"

"I didn't say that either. I mean we don't allow cheating on this ship."

"What about his partner over there?" He nodded his head in the direction of the man in the white suit, who was still at the roulette table.

The man looked O'Reilly over. "You don't miss much. We don't either."

He decided to drop it. He'd done his boy scout duty for the evening. He didn't like the ominous way the man implied he was going to take care of the problem, but that wasn't his business.

He was employed to find the ship owner's daughter, not protect his gambling profits.

O'Reilly nodded his head. "Be seeing you," he said, walking off.

Chapter 12

"I imagine that Tony Braga, that's the guy in charge of the high-stakes gaming room, will have a talk with the man in the tuxedo later, perhaps in his cabin," Captain Firestone said. They were at his private table, set apart from the other tables in the ship's main dining room. "That gaming room is a world unto itself. Braga reports directly to Martini. He has authority over whatever happens there, and I keep my nose out of it."

"You're the captain. You're legally responsible for everything that happens on the ship, right? That's why you're getting blamed for Martini's daughter's disappearance." O'Reilly had ordered another gin and tonic, and Firestone was sipping on a red wine. They were waiting for their steaks, which they had ordered from *Latitude*, the ship's premier steakhouse, not the main dining room where they sat—an option available only to the Captain and his guests.

"Of course. But the people who use that room are special guests of Martini or of friends of his: guys like that old man in the jogging outfit you mentioned and the business group the man at the bar was part of. They're invited here to gamble, and they often don't even stay for the whole voyage. Martini himself comes aboard sometimes and acts as host. He may even gamble with them. If the men who cheated were his guests, they won't be welcome on any of the ships anymore—and not on anyone else's line either."

The Captain stopped talking. He was staring across the dining room. "Isn't that Phyllis, your ex-wife over there?" he asked, avoiding pointing but directing his gaze toward a woman and man, who had gotten up and were definitely heading in their direction.

O'Reilly's expression turned glum. "I forgot to tell you," he answered. "Phyllis is on this ship. Phyllis and a cop who's a certified asshole."

The couple was still walking toward them, the woman eagerly, the man being pulled along by her insistent hand.

"That's who she's with? A cop?"

"He steals a lot of money. She likes that."

The couple had reached them and Captain Firestone stood up. Phyllis threw her arms around him. "Ted, it's been years. I had no idea you were Captain of this ship. This is wonderful." She smiled sweetly down at O'Reilly, who hadn't gotten up and was frowning. Then she turned to her partner. "Ted, this is Derrick Sterling. We're together. Derrick, Ted is the Captain; isn't that wonderful?"

Sterling took a step forward to shake the Captain's outstretched hand. The burly policeman barely managed a smile as he kept glancing down at O'Reilly sitting at the table.

"Derrick is an important guest, Captain. He's a big time extortionist back home," O'Reilly said, a cheery smile returning to his face. "Just don't let him around any of your third world crew members. He'll take their money."

"Shut your big mouth, scumbag," Sterling growled. He was staring down at O'Reilly with fire in his eyes.

"Come on boys, can't we be friends for just tonight?" Phyllis said, looking from one of them to the other, her tone that of a kindergarten teacher disciplining two rambunctious children. She looked back at Captain Firestone. "Brian says he's leaving the ship tomorrow, is that right, Captain?"

"Brian is doing some important work for us," Firestone answered. "He'll be continuing that work on land, starting tomorrow."

"Then you two can play without me looking over your shoulder," O'Reilly said. "You can even pretend to be respectable, Derrick, and no one on board will be the wiser... unless they get to know you."

Sterling continued to stare at him and grind his teeth but he didn't say anything.

"Well I'm glad to see you again, Phyllis," the Captain said. 'Maybe we can have dinner together, some night... you and Mr. Sterling." He glanced down at O'Reilly. "It'll probably be more pleasant without so many... irritants around." He gave a brief smile as he gazed at O'Reilly.

Phyllis and Sterling said their goodbyes and left. Firestone sat down and gave O'Reilly a withering look. "Really, Brian?"

"The guy's a dishonest cop who bullies whoever can't defend himself. He pulls in lots of money, most of it acquired dishonestly, and Phyllis loves it. She doesn't care where the money comes from, as long as it's there."

"Do you think you might be a little biased?"

"Damn straight, I'm biased. I don't like dishonest cops and Sterling is the epitome of the dishonest cop."

Firestone shot him a skeptical look. "I meant because of Phyllis."

"Phyllis and I are history. I don't like the kind of person she is, but after ten years of marriage, I understand her. And I don't want to cause her any grief. It's a good thing I'm leaving the ship tomorrow, because if I stayed, I'd just have to beat the shit out of Sterling."

"So you're completely over Phyllis?"

"One hundred percent."

Firestone slowly nodded his head, a half smile on his face. "I'm one hundred percent reassured."

"Good," O'Reilly said. "Now can we get back to what I was hired to do?"

"Of course," Firestone answered between bites of his steak. "So you'll be getting off in Toulon tomorrow. You're done talking to the crew?"

"I'm meeting Anka Sokolov tonight in the crew's bar and she's going to introduce me to some others who knew Julietta,."

"Ah, Anka…" Firestone smiled. "I know which one Anka is. Everybody does. You wouldn't be just looking for some extra time with her, would you?" His face broke into his signature grin.

"I have a very strict work ethic," O'Reilly answered, straight-faced. "I never want to put something to bed until I'm sure I've exhausted it." He looked up from his meal and his face broke into a grin. "I don't know how hard it's going to be to exhaust Anka."

"You're forty-one years old, pardner. She's what, twenty-five or six?" Firestone told him. "You'll be exhausted long before she is."

APPOINTMENT IN MYKONOS

Chapter 13

The rich girl was a pain in the ass. Marina had gone along with everything in her usual meek way, trusting Dmitri right up to the point that he had locked her in her room in Vucovic's brothel. The rich girl had been a different story. She had been suspicious from the start, complaining when Dmitri said he was taking them to a friend's house in *Szentendr*e, a village outside of Budapest, threatening to call her rich father to send someone for her. Dmitri had finally had to drug her drink to keep her quiet.

Once they were in the house in *Szendtendre*, Marina still followed all of Dmitri's orders, even swallowing the story that Goran and Filip were his cousins. She wondered why her rich friend was sleeping through everything, but Dmitri had told her that he thought the other girl might be sick. He even said he was going to have his cousin call a doctor. It was only when he locked Marina in her room that she realized that she had been kidnapped.

The rich friend was something else. She woke up in one of the brothel's bedrooms and immediately started pounding on the door to be let out. When Dmitri opened the door, the girl had jumped on him and actually tried to scratch his face, calling him a "pervert," and a "pimp." She yelled at him that her father would send men to find her, that he had friends who would kill Dmitri if he didn't let her go. Perhaps she was right, but her rich father would never know where she was. Dmitri had told her to shut up and he'd had to sock her in the mouth to try to make her quiet. When that hadn't stopped her he had given her a real beating.

The rich bitch still hadn't been with a man. Every time she woke up, she started screaming and no matter how many times Dmitri or even Goran hit her, she came back for more. Finally they decided to just keep her sedated until she gave up. Who knew how long that would take?

Vucovic was pissed at him for bringing along someone who caused that much trouble. He told Dmitri that he would give the girl three days and if she didn't calm down by then, if she continued to attack whoever approached her and hadn't earned any money, then Dmitri would have to get rid of her—permanently—and find a replacement.

Shit! Dmitri had never killed anyone… well, not if you didn't count the two whores whom he had killed by accident. And how was he going to find another girl? Go on another cruise ship? He wasn't going to hang around Naples again, not after the *Camorra* figured out that he had kidnapped someone right under their noses.

He would have to get the rich girl to start cooperating. That meant a lot more beatings.

APPOINTMENT IN MYKONOS

Chapter 14

Anka had changed out of her Maître d's uniform and was wearing a knit dress, gathered over one shoulder and leaving the other shoulder bare, belted at the waist and stopping mid-thigh—which showed off her smooth, nicely rounded legs. The thin knit material, when she turned to the side, with the light behind her, yielded a mouth-watering view of her ample and unsupported breasts. Seated at her table in the crew's bar were two other young women, both in jeans shorts and blouses and a young man in jeans and a tee shirt.

"You look even more beautiful than when I talked to you this afternoon," O'Reilly told Anka, sitting down next to her. He had left his seersucker sport coat in his cabin and was wearing suntan slacks and a short-sleeved polo shirt, revealing his long muscular arms with their Southern California tan. "She doesn't know what she does to an old man," he joked, turning to the other three people at the table. "This could be a dangerous evening for me. I hope someone is trained in CPR."

The others at the table laughed.

"Mr. O'Reilly thinks he is old," Anka said to her companions. "He does not know what old is. A week on a cruise ship among passengers in their eighties and nineties and he will think he is hardly more than a teenager."

The others laughed again. O'Reilly was encouraged, but he wasn't sure that Anka wasn't being extra nice to him because of his relationship with the Captain. She was an ambitious young woman.

"These are your friends who knew Julietta?" he asked Anka.

"Natasha was pretty close with Julietta and Maria was a friend of Marina. Jimmy shared a cabin with Dmitri."

O'Reilly shook hands all around and ordered a gin and tonic. The young people at the table were all drinking beer, except Anka, who was sipping a glass of red wine. He began by asking Natasha what she knew about Julietta. She was a black-haired young woman, who, like most of the other crew appeared to be in her mid-twenties, was modelishly slim, with large, dark, sad eyes set above high cheekbones. She had a long, narrow nose and a wide mouth, which turned down at the corners, as if she were holding in a deep melancholy. She looked at O'Reilly with a trusting gaze.

"You are really an American detective?" she asked, her English flavored by a strong Eastern European accent.

He nodded. "I'm an American private detective, working right now for Seven Seas Cruise Line and I'm looking for Julietta Martini." He was trying to maintain a serious expression, even though his thoughts were bouncing like a teenager's attention span between Natasha's slim figure and Anka's voluptuous one. "Did she say anything to you about her plans in Naples or about returning or not returning to the ship?"

"She told me that she was tired of being on the ship and she was going ashore to have lunch at a café and walk around the town. She didn't talk as if she would be on shore very long."

"She didn't say she was planning to visit anyone?"

The young woman shook her head. "No."

He was disappointed. Tracing Julietta's contacts in Naples was going to be difficult unless she'd mentioned a name to someone.

"Marina probably knew," Maria, the other female crew member offered. She was a plain looking olive-skinned girl, a little overweight and who, O'Reilly guessed, was Italian. She had a serious face but looked down at the table after she had spoken, as if she were embarrassed.

"Julietta and Marina were friends?" he asked, looking at each one of the young crew members.

Anka and Natasha shook their heads and the male, Jimmy, shrugged noncommittally.

"They weren't good friends, but they knew each other," Maria answered, meeting his gaze before she looked down again. "I know they left the ship together."

"Together?" Another revelation.

"I said goodbye to Marina right before she got off the ship," Maria continued. "She was waiting for Julietta."

"But they weren't really friends?" Again he was asking the group.

Both Anka and Natasha looked as if they were surprised by Maria's claim. They shook their heads again.

"They knew each other, but not well," Maria said. "Marina told me that Julietta had offered to share a taxi to take her to her house." She paused then looked uncomfortably toward the other two women. "I don't think they planned to do anything together. They weren't that kind of friends. It was more of a favor that Julietta was doing for Marina, who didn't have a lot of money."

"And Dmitri? I kind of assumed that Marina and Dmitri left the ship together," O'Reilly said.

Jimmy, who had been Dmitri's cabin-mate still looked blank but Maria answered. "I saw Dmitri waiting for Marina on the dock."

"Do you think Julietta was sharing a taxi with both of them—Marina and Dmitri?"

Maria nodded. "I think so."

"Did Dmitri mention any of this to you?" he asked Jimmy.

Jimmy shook his head. He was a good-looking young man in his mid-twenties with curly black hair and dark eyes, probably from one of the Eastern European countries. He was well-built and was wearing just a white tee-shirt on top, which revealed his well-muscled shoulders and biceps. "He didn't talk to me much, except when he first came on board and was asking about which female crew were unmarried and without boy friends."

"And you told him."

Jimmy smiled and flashed his dark eyes at the three women. "Sure. That's a normal question from new male crew members."

"Did you tell him about Marina? Was she one of the ones you mentioned?"

He nodded, looking embarrassed. "I didn't think he'd go for her though. She was too shy and she didn't like to party."

Dragic sounded like a typical predator to O'Reilly. If he zeroed in on Marina then the man had been looking for the most vulnerable females from the time he arrived on the ship. "What else can you tell me about Dmitri?"

Jimmy shrugged. "He was a jerk as far as I'm concerned. He kept his side of the cabin like a pigsty; he was drunk every night, and every time I worked with him he was late for his shift. If he hadn't jumped ship he probably would have gotten fired."

"Did he talk about Marina or Julietta?"

Jimmy sneered. "I saw him around Julietta. He acted like he thought she was God's gift to the world, sucking up to her, trying to put moves on her. She saw right through him, though. Anyone could see that. And in private he called her a 'bitch.' He said she'd get what was coming to her for acting so high and mighty. He said her money couldn't always protect her."

"You mean he threatened her?"

"Not to her face. He was always super-nice around her, at least as much as he could be, given he was an asshole with the manners of a bum. But when he got drunk and talked in the cabin, he went on and on about how she was going to get paid back someday."

"How about Marina. What did he say about her?"

"He called her 'that stupid bitch.' He bragged that he could get her to do anything." He looked around at his fellow crew members. "Listen mister, I knew Dmitri as well as anyone, and I thought he was a total scumbag. I didn't say anything to Julietta because I didn't really know her, and she looked like she knew Dmitri was an asshole anyway. But I warned Marina to stay away from him. She wouldn't listen. She thought he was wonderful. The fucking dirtbag knew how to turn on the charm when he wanted to, and that's what he did whenever he was around Marina. She wouldn't listen to anyone about him."

"Jimmy's right," Maria chimed in. "I tried to tell Marina that Dmitri was no good, but she was totally gonzo over him. She wouldn't listen to anyone."

"Great," O'Reilly said. "You can't imagine how much help this information is going to be."

"You mean it will help you find Julietta?" Anka asked, looking at him with even more respect than she'd had already.

He loved her adoration, but he didn't want to distort things, especially when he knew these young people cared about Julietta. "It gives me a place to start. It sounds as if Marina was the last person to see her, so I'll start with her." He looked around at them, his expression serious. "How much of what you told me tonight did you tell Magetti, the security man who works for Julietta's father?"

Natasha, Maria and Jimmy looked at each other. Each of their faces was blank. "He didn't talk to any of us," Natasha answered. "Right?" She scanned the faces of her fellow crew members. The other two nodded.

O'Reilly didn't say anything. Magetti's so-called investigation of Julietta's disappearance was laughable. But that just meant that it put more weight on his own efforts. That was fine with him. He didn't feel a lot differently than he did working in LA alongside of the LAPD, which was as unhelpful a partner as Magetti was turning out to be.

He shrugged his shoulders, then put on his most charming face. "Now how about I show all of you my appreciation by buying us all another round of drinks or two?"

The five of them had a few more rounds, and then Jimmy, Natasha and Maria excused themselves, saying they had to get to bed in order to be up for early morning breakfast shifts.

"How about you?" O'Reilly asked Anka.

"Another glass of wine will do me just fine. I'm not tired yet, are you?"

"I'm still on a different time schedule. My days and nights are out of whack. But don't you have to work in the morning?"

"It's a perk of being a Maître d'. My dining room isn't open in the morning. I start around eleven and help the chef supervise the supplies for the kitchen."

"I hadn't realized that a Maître d' had anything to do with the kitchen," O'Reilly said.

"They usually don't," she answered cheerily. "I asked for the job. If I want to be manager, I have to learn everything about the operation of the restaurant. That includes the kitchen more than anything else. I even attend the cooking lessons that the chefs give to the passengers." She beamed with pride.

"You *are* a go-getter," he said. "I hope you can sandwich in some time for me on your climb to the top."

"Don't be a sexist cynic," she answered, smiling sweetly. "Just because I want the same things any ambitious male in the work world would want, doesn't mean I don't covet your body." She looked his long, lean body up and down, then lowered her eyelids before returning her gaze to his face and giving him a raunchy wink.

Did he just get lucky? He wasn't about to look a gift horse in the mouth. He held up his glass in a toast. "Here's to shattering the glass ceiling. How about we have the next drink in my cabin?"

"That's what I like about mature men. You always have the best ideas."

He signaled the waiter then paid the tab and they left the bar. He'd done a lot of good investigating tonight… and now he was about to receive his reward. He could even get to like being known as "mature."

Chapter 15

The trip to Naples by air from Marseilles had taken four hours, including a change of planes in Rome. O'Reilly's mind had been on his night with Anka as much as on the task ahead of him. It was hard not to think of her. She was a beautiful, bright girl and they had hit it off wonderfully, both socially and sexually. He was acutely aware of their age difference, even though she claimed that it was of no consequence. But as the plane descended to the Naples airport, he put his romantic musings aside and switched his thoughts to the job of finding Julietta Martini.

He arrived in the seaport metropolis in the early afternoon and took a taxi from the airport into the heart of the city. Ahead of him, reaching toward the cloudless azure sky were enough skyscrapers to qualify Naples as the major city that it was, having the second largest metropolitan population in the country. The airport was near the spacious *Capodimente Park*, a welcome expanse of green amidst the crowded streets of the city. *Capodimente Park* was one of the largest and most picturesque urban green spaces in all of Italy and included its own Palace and wide boulevards as well as a small, dense forest. As they passed the park and looked down on the city, O'Reilly could see Mount Vesuvius in the distance, its infamous slopes descending to the sea. Despite its modern skyline, the heart of the city was reminiscent of its baroque heritage. Streets were narrower than in the U.S. and the buildings—most of them four or five stories tall—were covered in as much gingerbread as a Viennese pastry. The cab driver was justifiably proud of his city and O'Reilly found himself cruising by the city's main square, the *Piazza del Plebescito*, built, he learned from the driver, in the early 19th century as a tribute to Napoleon, who was the King of Naples' brother-in-law. The square was enormous and at one end of it was the impressive Romanesque church of *San Francesco di Paola* with its dozens of marble columns. Across the square stood the more staid, Royal Palace, once the home of the city's Bourbon Kings, but now the location of the *Teatro di San Carlo*, the city's opera house. He thanked the cab driver for the brief history lesson then instructed him to take him to *Mercato*, the site of the medieval market area of the city, which was a quarter near the industrial port area and the home of the city's sizeable Polish immigrant community, a community which included the family of Maria Stepovich.

Marina Stepovich's family had told Captain Firestone that their daughter had arrived at their house in the Mercato quarter the day the ship had docked in Naples. She had been accompanied by Dmitri, but not Julietta, although she had mentioned that another woman had shared the taxi with them. Marina and Dmitri had eaten lunch with her family but had departed soon after. Marina had insisted on accompanying the young man she was with to Budapest, where he had said there would be jobs waiting for both of them. With Neapolitan unemployment approaching 25%, and even higher among non-Italians, including Marina's Polish-born father, her parents could not keep their daughter from leaving. That was five days ago, and there had been no word from her since, despite her promise to call them as soon as she arrived in Budapest.

Marina's family's home was on the second floor of a cheaply constructed wooden tenement on a busy street of one and two story wooden buildings, mostly shops advertising their wares in both Polish and Italian. Despite its poverty, it was a vibrant neighborhood. Many of the merchants displayed their products on the sidewalk in large bins or tables, each of them heaped with clothing, shoes, fresh fruit, even sausages and fish. The streets were crowded, mostly with shoppers on foot, mostly women in headscarves carrying cloth shopping bags on their arms.

O'Reilly found the address and climbed the dark staircase to the Stepovich's second floor apartment and knocked on the door. It was opened by a middle-aged man with a day's growth of beard, who stood with a marked stoop and stared at O'Reilly with suspicion. O'Reilly showed the man and his wife his Seven Seas Cruise Line ID card and explained that he was a representative of the ship and that he was following up on the Captain's phone call to try to make sure that he knew where Marina was and how to contact her in order to extend her another contract for employment on the *Adriatic Voyager*. He explained that Marina's work had been outstanding, and the company did not like to lose such a valuable employee. Both parents nodded appreciatively at the praise for their daughter, but it did not overcome their anxiety about her whereabouts.

"This Dimitri, he was also an employee?" Marina's father asked. He walked with a limp that he said he got from an accident when he was working on the docks. He had an animated face, which showed his friendliness, once he knew that O'Reilly was there to help, although his eyes were haggard from worry. He was bitter about being unemployed, which he claimed was partly because of the economy and partly because of his disability but also because he wasn't Italian and, despite his Polish contacts within the union, almost all the jobs during this economic recession were now going to native born Italians. The couple's only daughter had been an important source of income for the family, which was one of the reasons that he and his wife had given in to letting her accompany Dmitri to Budapest.

O'Reilly was unsure how much he should tell them about Dragic. He didn't want to alarm them, even though he was pretty sure that whatever their daughter had been lured into by the young Serb was going to end up being disastrous for her. "Dimitri was only with the ship for a few weeks," he finally said. "He was not so valuable to us as your daughter. It is her that I am looking for. Did she say anything about where she planned to stay in Budapest… or did Dmitri?"

The father looked at his wife, a heavy-set woman with graying hair, who could barely conceal the panic in her dark eyes. She blinked back tears that threatened to course down her puffy cheeks and onto the faded blue front of her large, formless housedress. She shrugged her shoulders and gave her husband a blank look. He turned to O'Reilly and shook his head sadly. "She talked about finding a hotel first and then getting an apartment after she found work. I think the boy had family there. He said he was from Budapest and knew many people."

"Did either of them talk about the woman they shared the cab ride with?" The fate of Marina was troubling, but his priority was finding Julietta.

The two parents looked at each other, uncertainly.

"Marina and the young man had a disagreement about another person. They didn't say her name. They argued, although Marina finally gave in."

"A disagreement about what?"

"The boy—Dimitri—he wanted to find the other young woman and take her to Budapest with them. Marina said the woman was rich. She didn't need a job. But the boy said that Marina's friend could just come along to keep Marina company. He said she'd have a good time in Budapest and Marina wouldn't be lonely."

"And Marina finally agreed?"

The father looked at his wife. "Marina is not very strong. She works hard and is a good daughter, but she can't stand up to other people. This Dmitri, he insisted very much."

"And so they left? In a taxi?"

Mr. Stepovich nodded. "We don't have a car. Marina would have taken the bus, but the young man said they needed to go straight to the airport after they found the other woman."

O'Reilly stood and thanked them. "This has been very helpful."

The mother stepped forward. She raised her eyes to his face. They were pleading. "You will look for Marina? We're afraid something has happened to her. I did not like this boy, Dmitri."

O'Reilly felt at a loss. His job was to find Julietta Martini, not Marina Stepovich. But Marina's parents were distraught, and whatever had happened to their daughter might also be the fate of Julietta. At least, it was the strongest lead he had so far. "I will try," he said. "I can't promise anything, but I'll go to Budapest and see what I can find out."

Both parents reached out and grasped his hands in theirs. "Thank you," the mother said, her tears finally pouring full force down her round cheeks. The father nodded his head and looked O'Reilly in the eyes. "We appreciate what you are doing," he said. "We want our daughter back."

O'Reilly left the apartment feeling guilty. He hoped he hadn't given Marina's parents false hope. Marina and Julietta might have shared the same fate, but, if so, it was one that would make tracking them down extremely difficult. And even if they were taken together, there was no guarantee that they had ended up together in Budapest or anywhere else. He needed more information on Dragic and where he was known to hang out in Budapest—a city with which O'Reilly was completely unfamiliar. That meant he needed to find the man who was most likely to have that information: Sergio Magetti. He had Magetti's cell phone number, and he made the call as soon as he got down the stairs and out onto the sidewalk.

Magetti was in Budapest.

Chapter 16

The door slammed and Marina lay on the bed, shaking with both fear and shame. She listened to the steps receding down the hallway, then lowered herself to the floor. She wasn't sure that she could stand. The drugs with which she'd been injected had made her dizzy. Her legs would not obey her will, as if they belonged to someone else. She leaned forward and pushed herself up with her hands until she was sitting on her haunches. She reached a hand over to the bed to steady herself, then waited to catch her breath.

She felt dirty... and stupid. How could she have believed that Dmitri loved her? Or that she loved him? He was an animal. She still had his sweaty smell all over her. She tried to breathe through her mouth so she wouldn't smell him. She gasped for air. She looked down. The fluids that he had left inside of her were oozing down her leg, forming a small pool on the floor. With an effort she used the bed to stand. Unsteadily she teetered toward the door, grasping its knob as if it were a lifebuoy on the sea. The knob wouldn't turn.

It had been three days now since she had been brought into the room by Dmitri, him telling her that it was his cousin's house and they would stay there while they looked for jobs. But as soon as he had left the room, she had realized that she could not open the door. And where was her friend? Her friend had slept all the way from the airport to the house. Dmitri has said that she was sick. His cousin was going to call a doctor. But the cousin and another man had taken her friend to another room and she had not seen her again. There were only the screams from down the hall.

When Dmitri had returned that first day, he had told her that they should make love. He'd said they were a couple and they were alone and he was lonely. She had refused. Then he had hit her. He had forced himself on her. The more she'd fought him, the harder he'd hit her, until she'd finally given in.

"You don't love me," she had told him afterward.

"I don't need to love you to fuck you," he had answered, his face serious. "You need to learn to fuck better. Many men will come here and they will want a good time. You will give them a good time or I will beat you."

Her first reaction had been shock. Then shame… shame for having had sex with Dmitri but even more, shame for being so naïve. She had heard of girls being kidnapped for prostitution. Her parents had warned her. She had never been able to imagine such a thing happening to herself. She was too cautious, too careful. But she had believed Dmitri and now she knew that she was stupid.

He had been back. Each time he had forced her to have sex with him; told her not to tell anyone or he would beat her, maybe kill her. He bragged that he had killed two girls already. She was terrified; she did whatever he asked.

Then the other men started coming. They were older than Dmitri. Older and fatter… but cleaner. They'd made her perform… do things she had never imagined were done between a man and a woman. When she'd refused, they would call for Dmitri or one of the other men, Goran or Filip, and she would be threatened. If she still refused, she would be hit until she complied. And still, Dmitri came during the day.

She had asked about her friend. Dmitri had only laughed. He showed her his skinned knuckles. "That is from hitting your friend. She is a bitch. She thinks she is too good to be a whore. I showed her. Goran too. We showed her."

"Is she alive?" Marina had been afraid to ask the question, but she was afraid not to. It had been her fault that her friend was here. She had begged her to come with her to Budapest. She had thought it would make her feel safer, less lonely.

"She is alive for now, but if she does not cooperate as you are, she will be dead soon," Dmitri had answered. "Vucovic, my boss has given her one more day. If she still fights us, she will be killed."

"I want to see her," Marina had told him.

"Why?"

"To tell her to do what you say. To tell her that I have given in to you. She has to do it or she will die." Her eyes had been pleading.

"OK."

He had taken her down the hall to her friend's room. Her friend was lying on the bed, naked. She raised her head. One eye was nearly closed and blue from a bruise. Her upper lip was swollen. There were large dark bruises over her kidneys.

Dmitri had left them alone.

Marina had begged her friend to stop resisting. They would get away sometime, but for now, she had to do what Dmitri and the others asked of her or they would kill her.

"I will never do that," her friend had said. Tears ran down her cheeks but her eyes blazed in defiance.

"You have to. Dmitri says they will kill you. "Marina gulped before continuing. "I have done what they want. I have had sex with several men. I hate it but I don't want to die or be beaten."

Her friend had bent over and covered her face in her hands. She began to sob.

Dmitri walked into the room. "OK, that's it. Back to your room, Marina." He had grabbed her by the arm and begun pulling her to the door. "You'd better listen to your friend, bitch," he had told the other woman. She was still sobbing and hadn't looked up.

That had been this morning. This afternoon Dmitri had come back to have sex with her. When she had asked about her friend, he had just laughed. "Everybody gives in. Your friend is not so strong as she thinks. Now she will find out what it means to be a whore." When he had left her he was still laughing.

She let go of the door handle and stumbled back to the bed. At least her friend would not be killed. Somehow they would get out of this. She knelt beside the bed and began to pray.

Chapter 17

The *Hotel Palazzo Zichy*, built at the end of the 19th century as the city palace of Count Nandor Zichy, whose statue stood across the street, was a four-star hotel in the "palace" section of Budapest, a short walk from the downtown district on the *Pest* side of the Danube. The Count had been a wealthy and, in his youth rebellious, nobleman whose business and political achievements had made him a central feature of Budapest city life during the late 1800s. O'Reilly had learned about the Count and his palatial home from the cab driver as he sped down the narrow two-lane road which led from the *Franz Liszt Airport* through the fertile farmland that surrounded the city, toward the downtown. "It is one of three palaces of the Zichy family in our city," the driver told him. "It's not the nicest of Budapest's palaces, but it is surely one of the nicest to be turned into a hotel. You are here as a tourist?"

"A pleasure tourist," O'Reilly answered. "I hear there are lots of places to find young women in this city." He figured that he might as well begin his search immediately. Cabbies knew everything that went on below the surface of a city's respectable façade.

The driver eyed him in the rear-view mirror. O'Reilly hoped he looked the part of a profligate, middle-aged American. He wasn't stretching the truth very far.

"You want me to show you where to find women?"

"That's what I'm here for."

The man eyes remained on him in the mirror. "Women are not hard to find in Budapest. We have strip clubs, escort services. They advertise in the papers, even on TV. Even the tour guides will take you to the strip clubs."

"I have unusual interests. I'm looking for something more private, less… regulated."

The driver's expression became suspicious. "You are an American. How do you know we have such things?"

"A friend told me. An American friend. He was here about a year ago. He said he visited a place run by Bosnians, Serbians, whatever … I don't remember exactly. He said anything goes at a place like that."

"Maybe such places exist..." The driver's suspicion was echoed in his voice.

"You could take me there… if they exist?"

"A place like that… it's not legal. I cannot take you."

O'Reilly figured that the driver thought he might be a policeman. "You're afraid I'm a cop?"

"You're not fat enough to be a Hungarian cop."

O'Reilly laughed. "I'm not any kind of cop. So can you take me to one of those places?"

"Not me, but I have a friend."

"How do I contact your friend?"

The driver fumbled inside of his jacket pocket for a few seconds and then pulled out a card. He reached over the seat and handed it to O'Reilly. The card had a telephone number written on it."

"Who do I ask for?"

"Jerzy. Ask for Jerzy. He will meet you and you can tell him what you want."

"Thanks," O'Reilly said. He tucked the card inside of his wallet.

"We're at your hotel," the driver announced.

The taxi had pulled to the curb. A liveried doorman opened the cab door. "Welcome to Hotel, Palazzo Zichy," he greeted O'Reilly.

Although it had once been a "palace," the hotel building was really an enormous, square, town residence, which took up nearly all of a city block. It was tucked away on a narrow side street across from a small plaza, which contained the statue of the hotel's namesake. On another corner was a small, baroque-looking Catholic church. Despite its 19th century façade, the inside of the hotel was sleek and modern. To one side of the lobby was an elegant bar and behind the registration desk O'Reilly could glimpse a sunken restaurant on the floor below. He glanced around and found the elevator off to one side of the lobby, next to what appeared to be a reading room with plush leather chairs and carpets.

He took the elevator to the fourth floor then walked down the hall until he found room 438, the number the operator had given him over the phone when he'd called from Naples. He knocked on the door.

The door was opened by a short, muscular man, wearing a too-tight suit, which seemed ready to burst at the seams over his large shoulders and biceps. He looked O'Reilly over without expression. "What can I do for you?" he asked.

"Tell Magetti that O'Reilly's here." When the man turned around O'Reilly brushed by him into the room.

Sergio Magetti was sitting at a desk typing on a laptop. When he looked up, his face showed his surprise. "What are you doing here?" he asked. The muscle bound security man at the door had scurried around to place his compact body between O'Reilly and his boss.

"Tell Arnold Schwarzenegger to move and we can talk," O'Reilly said.

"Ducati, go back to the door," Magetti ordered. The man shrugged and walked back toward the door, then sat down in a chair about three feet away from the room's entrance and stared straight ahead.

"So now we can talk. What are you doing here?" Magetti asked him again. He looked irritated.

"I thought you missed me," O'Reilly answered. "Mind if I sit down?"

Magetti closed his laptop with a sigh. "Go ahead," he said, motioning toward a couch in the

111

middle of the room. "I thought you were going to work solo."

"I was, but I was missing a necessary piece of the music," O'Reilly answered, leaning toward the Italian. "I need to know what you know about Dmitri Dragic."

Magetti had turned his chair to face the couch. "So you're ready to admit that Dragic took Julietta." He couldn't suppress a smile.

"He took a woman from the ship. Whether or not he took both her and Julietta, is still not clear to me."

Magetti stared at him. "What do you mean he took a woman? You mean someone else?"

"Marina Stepovich."

Magetti sat back, his face skeptical. "Who the hell is Marina Stepovich?"

"A crew member on the *Adriatic Voyager*. She and Dragic and Julietta shared a taxi when they left the ship. Dragic had lunch with Marina's family in Naples. Then he and Marina flew here. They may or may not have taken Julietta with them."

Magetti stared hard at him. "How did you find all this out?"

"I did what you should have done. I interviewed the crew and I talked to Marina's parents in Naples."

Magetti's eyes flashed in irritation and he looked ready to challenge him but stopped himself and rubbed his chin thoughtfully. "So Dragic is with this Marina here in Budapest. We knew he came here but that's about all. We haven't been able to find any trace of Julietta so we're trying to locate Dragic."

"You must have some information about his hangouts, his friends, his business associates. That's what I need to know."

Magetti's hostility had returned. "Why should I share it with you?"

O'Reilly heaved a sigh. "Don't be an ass Magetti. I just shared a shitload of information with you about Dragic and about Marina Stepovich. I'm not trying to be cagey. I want Julietta found. Whatever I know, I'll turn it over to you, whatever you know, I expect the same from you."

Magetti was still thinking. Finally he blew out his breath and looked up at O'Reilly. "OK. Dragic has family here in Budapest: an uncle and a cousin. He lived with them when he was here. Both of them are known to be involved in prostitution. Not the street kind, but illegal brothels, operated in the suburbs on the edge of the city where there isn't much surveillance or concern about what goes on."

O'Reilly grinned at him. "Now don't you feel better—sharing information instead of hoarding it all to yourself? You've got addresses for his relatives and for these brothels?"

Magetti had to suppress his irritation, but he nodded. "We have addresses for his cousin and his uncle's house but only two of the brothels. We have them under surveillance. So far neither Dragic nor Julietta has been seen at any of the locations.

"Waiting until he shows up is too slow. You've got addresses for two of the brothels he works with. There's no telling how many more brothels he has contacts with. How about we begin searching them?"

Magetti heaved another sigh. "We can't go in and search any of them. We have no authority."

"Who do you need to ask? Your boss? Your parents? Your girlfriend? These are brothels, you can visit them whenever you want."

Magetti looked uncomfortable. "We're not undercover agents."

"You're not but I am. I've done this kind of thing a lot. I used to work undercover for the Los Angeles Police Department." No need to mention that he'd also been fired from the LAPD.

"Are you suggesting that you're going to visit those two brothels?"

"Those two and every other one I can find. They're brothels. They're not going to be out of sight or they won't have any customers. I have a number for someone who can take me to one… run by Serbians or Bosnians."

Magetti stared at him. "You work quickly." Despite his irritation, he sounded impressed.

"I'm not on salary like some people."

"Maybe we should work together."

O'Reilly looked at Magetti's face. The man was clearly embarrassed to have made the suggestion after his insistence that O'Reilly would be in his way. O'Reilly smiled. "I thought you'd never ask."

114

Magetti nodded without smiling. "Good. We can keep up the surveillance on his relatives' house and you can try to get into the brothels. We can wait in the wings in case you run into any trouble."

He wanted to go in alone, but he didn't mind having Magetti standing by with the cavalry in case things got hairy once he was inside either of the brothels. "Sounds like a plan. When can you be ready?"

"Whenever you are."

"I'll take a taxi. Give me the addresses. You can be in the neighborhood and I'll call you on my cell phone if things start to go south."

"South?" Magetti's face showed his confusion.

"If I'm in trouble or I need help."

Magetti nodded again. He went over to the desk where he'd been typing and picked up a piece of paper. "We can go to the top one first; it's closer," he said, handing the slip of paper to O'Reilly.

O'Reilly took the paper. "Fine. Can you look up a taxi company in the phone book?" He didn't want to use the number given to him by the cab driver. He was saving him in case he needed to make more inquiries in the future. "Oh and, Magetti, I need one more thing."

The Italian heaved a sigh. "What is that?"

"A gun."

Magetti walked over to a thick hard-shell briefcase and opened it. Inside was a array of weapons. "No problem," he said. "Take your pick."

Chapter 18

The cab driver knew exactly the location of the first address. It was in a run-down area of old warehouses and industrial shops on the outskirts of the *Pest* section of the city. The building itself was a two-story apartment house, in somewhat better condition than the surrounding structures, with fresh white paint and a new asphalt tile roof and what looked to be a newly constructed front porch. O'Reilly got out and paid the driver, then waited until he'd driven off before he called Magetti. "I'm here and I'm going in."

"Watch yourself," Magetti cautioned him.

"Don't worry. I know my way around a whorehouse."

He'd thought about his plan in the back seat of the taxi on the way there. He needed to be able to see as many of the girls in the brothel as possible. If he found Julietta—or Marina for that matter—he planned to select her, then either figure a way to smuggle her out of the building or call Magetti and tell him to storm the building with his men.

He rang the doorbell. A thin young man in a cheap, shiny suit with slicked back black hair and an earring opened the door. The man smiled. "I help you?" he asked in broken English.

"The cab driver said… this was a place… " O'Reilly acted embarrassed. "Maybe it's the wrong address…"

The man opened the door. He smiled wider, revealing a missing bottom front tooth. "Not wrong place. You are looking for women?"

He nodded, still looking embarrassed, as if he was unsure whether or not to enter.

"C'mon, C'mon," the man said. "This right place. We have lots of women. You have good time."

O'Reilly entered the building.

They were in an entrance hall of the apartment building. Just to his right the door to an apartment was open and he could see several women dressed in slips or short dresses, sitting on couches. The man motioned for him to enter the apartment. "Girls… we have girls in here," the man said, gesturing for O'Reilly to enter.

He walked into the apartment. It was a living room and beyond a low counter he could see a small kitchen. A round table sat in the dining area, and a short, fat man in a wrinkled brown wool suit got up and came toward him. On one side of the living room were two empty easy chairs, both covered in cheap, fuzzy blue cloth. Across the floor were two couches set end to end. There were three girls on each. Another young woman was in the kitchen area, leaning over the counter eyeing him, appreciatively. One of the girls on the nearest couch looked up and smiled shyly. The others looked at the floor or stared straight ahead. They might have been drugged.

The short fat man stuck out his hand. "Welcome, you are very welcome here," he said, smiling broadly. He seemed genuinely pleased to see O'Reilly. "You will have a good time. I personally guarantee it."

O'Reilly shook the man's hand. "Is this all the girls you have?" he asked, disappointment in his voice.

The man laughed. "These girls? Of course not. These are just here for a...what do you call it? A teaser. We have many girls here."

"I'm looking for something special," O'Reilly said. "Young, but not a kid. Actually I'm looking for two girls. I want them to show me some things with each other." He looked hesitant. "I like to watch," he finally said.

"Sure, why not. Watching is half the fun... maybe more than half, eh? Our girls can do that for you, no problem. You just pick the girls you want to watch."

"Can I see the others?"

The man's face showed his dismay. "You don't like any of these girls? You haven't even taken a good look yet."

Neither Julietta nor Marina was one of the women. He wanted to see the others. "They're not my taste. Or maybe they are, but I want to see the others before I choose."

"No problem!" the man answered, his broad smile returning, as if O'Reilly's request was just what he had been hoping to hear. He turned toward the young man who had answered the door and had sat down at the round dining table and picked up a magazine. "Benny. Get to work! Go get the other girls and bring them for this gentleman to see."

Benny looked surprised. "All of them?"

"Every last one," the man exclaimed. He turned back to O'Reilly, a big grin on his face. "You want to make the very best choice, am I right?"

"Absolutely." O'Reilly grinned back.

In a few minutes Benny returned, trailing eight more young women, most of them looking even more drugged than the seven already in the room. Neither Julietta nor Marina was among them.

"Is that it?" O'Reilly asked.

The fat man looked at him sharply. "That is fifteen girls. Surely your taste cannot be more specialized than that."

"They look drugged."

The man looked offended. "Drugged? We do not do that my friend. These girls are just tired. It is the middle of the day and they do most of their work at night. They were all asleep until Benny woke them up."

O'Reilly gave him a skeptical look.

"You must choose now, mister," the fat man said. His voice had gained a hard edge. "We have gone to a lot of trouble for you. Now you must place an order, so-to-speak."

He was right. O'Reilly could have probably bulled his way out of the brothel, but the word would probably spread to other brothels owned by the same people and he would never be allowed into those places. He looked the women over, then picked two who appeared more alert than the others. "I'll take these two," he said.

"An excellent choice!" The man's ebullient spirit had revived.

O'Reilly followed the two women, whose names he learned were Monica and Serena. When they got to their room which was a bedroom in an upstairs apartment that otherwise appeared to be empty, he asked them to engage in lovemaking while he watched. Although they readily agreed, neither girl was much into her performance, and he waited politely and patiently until they were finished, then left them in the room and returned to the main floor.

"It was good, eh?" The fat man greeted him when he reached the bottom of the staircase.

"It was fine. The girls were great," O'Reilly answered, not wanting to register displeasure regarding the two women, fearing that they might be beaten if he hadn't been satisfied.

"Now you must pay. Each girl is five hundred Euros." The man looked at him with bright, greedy eyes.

"Five hundred each?" O'Reilly's shock was not feigned. "Who do you think these girls are? Angelina Jolie and Kate Upton?"

The man didn't seem to understand. He repeated his demand for a thousand Euros.

"You're nuts. I was with them less than a half-hour."

121

The man held out his hand as if he were helpless. "You could have stayed longer. It was up to you."

He had the money but he resented the robbery that paying such a price represented, even though he was playing a part by acting as a customer. He pulled out five one-hundred Euro bills. "Here's five hundred. And that's being generous."

The man looked at him. He was no longer smiling. "You don't want to do that, mister. We have to make a living here. We have fifteen girls to feed and clothe as well as ourselves. We don't like it when someone refuses to pay."

"I'm not refusing to pay, I just don't want to be robbed. Five hundred is a fair price for what I received."

"It is not you who sets the price." His eyes narrowed. "I am not fooling around. I can call Benny. Benny looks young and weak, but don't let his looks fool you, he knows how to hurt people."

"Benny couldn't hurt a fly." O'Reilly was getting angry with this pompous little fat man.

"Benny?" the man called. "Come and show this man what we do when someone won't pay us."

Benny emerged from one of the apartment's other rooms. He had a gun in his hand.

"Benny doesn't have to be very strong. He shoots very straight."

O'Reilly had a gun of his own under his coat and he knew that he could get the drop on Benny before he could get a shot off. But he would probably also have to shoot the fat man. Shooting two men in a country in which he was a guest, didn't sound wise. And he still had other brothels to visit.

"You win," he said, pulling another five bills out of his wallet.

The man's face broke into a grin. "I knew you were a reasonable man. Next time, if you return, spend more time with the girls… or ask for just one. The price will be more to your liking. Who knows, I may even give you a discount." He laughed.

O'Reilly wasn't laughing. Benny had gotten to within a few feet behind him and was still holding the gun, a shit-eating grin on his face. The two men's attitudes irked O'Reilly. In one quick motion he reached back and jerked the gun out of Benny's hand. Then he stuck it in the little fat man's face. "I'm willing to pay you, fatty, but don't have your hired cretin stick a gun in my face. OK?"

"OK," the fat man said, his eyes filled with fear.

"I'm glad we understand each other." O'Reilly said, emptying the gun and then handing it back to a terrified Benny. "Goodbye." He stepped outside and called Magetti on his cell phone.

Chapter 19

"You paid a thousand Euros to watch two women have sex?" Magetti asked, his mouth open in amazement. They were in Magetti's long black Mercedes, parked on a quiet road in a middle-class residential district about a block from the second brothel that Magetti had identified as one of those for which Dmitri Dragic worked.

"Don't knock it if you haven't tried it." O'Reilly answered, raising his eyebrows suggestively.

Magetti shook his head in disgust. "This is a serious investigation."

"Indeed it is," O'Reilly answered. "And I'm impersonating a customer at a whorehouse. What am I supposed to do? I have to pay for something, and these Serbians or Bosnians or whatever they are, are criminals. They get a customer in there and charge him five times what he should pay, then threaten his life if he doesn't pay up. I could pay less, and simply go with one of their girls, but then I'd probably get AIDS. Or I could shoot the two men instead of paying. Which of those options would you want me to choose?"

"OK, OK," Magetti said, holding up his hands in surrender. "So do you have enough money to do it again?"

"I do, but this is your boss' daughter, so you can pay this time. Besides, wouldn't you rather go instead of me? You might find it entertaining. I'll bet one of your men would jump at the chance."

"None of my men is going in there. You're the one who's doing it. I don't care what it costs. I'll give you the money."

"And I'll take it," O'Reilly said, holding out his hand. "Julietta is likely to be in one of these places and you're quibbling about paying a thousand Euros. I'll be back in less than an hour... or I'll call and you'd better be *there* in less than a minute."

"We'll be waiting right here," Magetti answered.

O'Reilly walked down the hill toward the house.

In forty minutes he was back.

"Same story. I'd say most of those girls are there against their will, but none of them is Julietta or Marina. They've got them drugged up... most of them anyway. That's a sure sign that they've been brought there involuntarily and are being kept there by being kept on drugs... probably beaten too, if they try to leave." O'Reilly paused and shook his head. "I'd love to shut this place down. It's a fucking disgrace that this country turns its back on this kind of thing."

"We're not here to save the world, O'Reilly. We're looking for one girl."

"You're looking for one. I'm looking for two."

"What do you mean?"

"Marina Stepovich. I'm sure Dragic sold her to one of these operations. I hope she's with Julietta, but whether she is or isn't, if I find her, I'm setting her free."

"That's not your job. It could jeopardize the whole search for Julietta."

"That's your problem. I've met Marina's parents. I told them I'd look for her. If I find her, I'm getting her out."

Magetti shook his head. "Jesus Christ. You're a fuckup, you know that?"

"And you're a pussy, so unless calling each other names is getting something accomplished, let's go find where the rest of these brothels are."

"How do we do that?"

'I've got to make contact with this guy who'll take me there." He took the card with the phone number on it then dialed the number on his cell phone. Someone with a low, gruff voice answered.

"Jerzy?" O'Reilly asked.

The man said something in what O'Reilly assumed was Hungarian.

"English. Speak English," O'Reilly told him.

"What do you want?"

"My taxi driver said you could take me to a Serbian brothel outside of town."

"What's your name?"

"O'Reilly."

"OK O'Reilly. I meet you at *Szimpla Kert*, one hour from now."

"*Szimpla Kert*? What's that?"

"Bar. Kazinczy street. One hour." The man hung up.

O'Reilly looked at Magetti. "Have you got a map?"

Magetti took a folded map the glove compartment and handed it to him. "What did he say?"

"He wants to meet me at some place called *Szimpla Kert* in an hour. It's a bar. Kazinscy street, wherever that is."

"Who is this guy?"

"Jerzy."

Magetti sighed. "Who the hell is Jerzy?"

O'Reilly was unfolding the map. "The guy my cab driver told me to call. He can take me to a brothel."

Magetti looked skeptical. "You're pretty trusting. How do you know this guy's legitimate?"

"He's not legitimate. And I don't trust him. But I haven't got a choice. The kind of brothel I asked for is illegal here. That's why it's out of town." He scoured the map. "Found it!" he exclaimed.

Chapter 20

He went in Magetti's car. He and the
security officer in the front and two of Magetti's
men in the back. *Szimpla Kert* was in a dilapidated
building on a street that seemed to be populated
mostly by bars and clubs. A small sign over a
narrow doorway identified the bar. Magetti parked
on the street a block away and O'Reilly walked
from there. "Follow me when I come out," he told
Magetti.

The inside of the bar was huge. He read a
sign on the wall that welcomed him in English to
"Budapest's Original *Ruin Pub*." Looking around,
he understood. The walls were old, brick, scarred
and damaged. Brick pillars ran from floor to ceiling.
Behind some of the pillars were smaller rooms,
some with their doorways crumbling. What
appeared to be cast-off furniture was scattered
haphazardly around the entire place. Posters and
pictures and graffiti adorned the walls. Various
floor and table lamps gave a soft amber glow, but
kept the bar in semi-darkness. At one end of the
main room bright sunlight was visible and a
courtyard with tables and umbrellas.

To his right as he walked in was a long bar.
Only one or two customers sat at it, but a group of
young men, who looked as if they were body
builders, all of them wearing skin-tight t-shirts that
showed off their sculpted bodies, were drinking and
talking loudly at a table in front of the bar. O'Reilly

approached the bartender, a burly young man with a huge belly, who wore a sleeveless undershirt and jeans and a workman's billed hat.

"I'm looking for Jerzy," O'Reilly said.

The bartender looked him up and down. "O'Reilly?"

He nodded.

"Upstairs and to the right on the second floor." The man pointed to a dark opening in the wall where the bottom of a staircase could just be made out.

He ordered a beer then carried it across the room and up the staircase. It went straight up and he emerged on the second floor in the middle of another large room with its own bar in one corner. An empty bandstand stood at the other end of the room. He turned right and saw a small room off to his right. A fat man in a black leather jacket sat drinking beer. He looked up and stared at O'Reilly as he approached the man.

"Jerzy?" O'Reilly asked.

"O'Reilly?"

"That's me." He took a seat opposite the man and put his beer on the table between them. "This is some kind of place."

"It's a good place to meet," the man said. "Quiet during the day. At night it's so busy you can't hear anyone talk. Music, girls, dancing. Lots of young people." He had a round, swollen face with small dark eyes. His black hair was thinning on top. A large beer belly stuck out from his leather jacket. He was wearing dark slacks and scuffed black

129

loafers. He eyes narrowed in suspicion. "Why don't you come here to find women. Lots of young women at night are here. Even whores."

O'Reilly shrugged. "Maybe I will. But right now I'm interested in something more unusual. A friend of mine told me about a brothel outside of town run by Serbians or Bosnians or something. My taxi driver said you could take me there"

The man's suspicious look hadn't left his face. "Maybe I can. I'm a taxi driver. I can take you wherever you want to go. It will cost you to go outside of town, though. I take you to a place, I don't know what you want there, what you do there, what kind of place it is. Understand?"

He understood that the man was trying to avoid entrapment in case O'Reilly was an undercover cop. "I understand. I tell you where I want to go and you just drive me there. Got it."

The fat man relaxed a little. He smiled, then picked up his beer and took a sip. "We finish our beers then we go, OK?"

"OK," O'Reilly answered. He watched as the man drained his glass. O'Reilly did the same. "Let's go," he said.

The man's cab was parked a block way from the bar. When they pulled away from the curb. O'Reilly glanced behind him to see the black Mercedes of Sergio Magetti pull out a block back. He hoped Magetti could follow him all the way, but if he couldn't he could call him when he got there and give him the address. Magetti shouldn't be far behind.

Chapter 21

At least the rich bitch had stopped attacking him. He'd finally broken her will. OK, so maybe it was Marina talking to her that had done the trick, but at least Vucovic was now off his back about bringing someone so well-connected back north with him. He'd told Vucovic that he hadn't known about the girl's father, even though that was a lie. In fact, having a rich father and acting as if she was better than Dmitri was what had made him determined to kidnap her. He knew that it was stupid. If he didn't know it, he had Vucovic there to tell him so, repeatedly.

But anyway, he was glad that he hadn't had to kill the bitch. He was even happier that he hadn't had to go out and find another girl. If Vucovic had sent him back to Naples, he would be dead meat. The girl's father must have already contacted the *Camorra* and told them that his daughter was missing. The *Camorra* had ears and eyes everywhere in Naples, and someone would recognize him as the one who'd left with the young woman. There was no way he could return to that city.

He had the last laugh on the girl's rich father, though. His little perfect daughter was no virgin. Dmitri had discovered that all by himself. Drugged and nearly unconscious from the beating that Goran had given her, the little bitch was in no shape to fight off Dmitri when he'd forced himself on her. That's when he knew that he wasn't the first

131

to have sex with her. Good thing he'd never told Vucovic that he was bringing back a virgin.

He'd raped her three more time since. Even when she'd been fully conscious, she'd no longer fought him. She hadn't acted as if she'd enjoyed it, but she'd learn to. Either that or she'd get more beatings. Dmitri liked beating women. It got him excited... almost as much as having sex. And she had to be trained, didn't she? She had to put on a performance for the brothel's guests. That's what they paid for.

Marina knew what to do. She was still shy, but she knew what was expected of her and she put out, like a good little whore. Dmitri had given her a few lessons. Not that Vucovic knew about it. He didn't know about the other one either. But Dmitri figured that taking his pleasure with the help ought to one of the perks of the job. And he knew that both Goran and Filip screwed the other girls whenever they pleased.

Poor stupid Marina. The first time he'd had sex with her, she'd thought he was in love with her. He guessed it was his good looks and charm having their usual effect. Of course, she'd realized what was what when he finished with her and told her she had to do better when she had a real customer. The dumb broad had almost flooded the room with her tears. And the wailing.... She wouldn't stop until he smacked her across the mouth. Then she'd shut up. And she'd looked at him with respect.

Of course it wasn't as good as getting that rich bitch to show him some respect. But that would come, even if it meant he had to beat her a few more times.

Chapter 22

The taxi drove to *Andrassy Avenue*. If Budapest was the "Paris of Eastern Europe," then the wide, tree-lined Andrassy Avenue was its Champs Elysee. The city's most prestigious shopping and dining street ran between *Erzsebet Square*, the massive park, lake and stopping place for every transit service and tour bus in the city and the beautiful *City Park*, crowned by the *Vajdahunyad Castle*, gracing the shores of the park's lake, which sported both colorful paddle boats and the elegant, neo-Baroque *Szechenyi Thermal Baths*. All of this was fronted by *Heroes' Square*, at the head of the avenue, with its statues of seven Magyar tribal chieftains. Driving down the elegant avenue, the driver skirted *Erzsebet Square* then passed the central business and shopping district of the *Pest* side of the city with its wide walking boulevards and sidewalk cafés before turning onto the graceful *Chained Bridge*, Budapest's first bridge across the Danube, designed and built by British engineers in the mid-19th century.

They climbed the Buda hills until they came to the *Buda Castle Tunnel*, built by the same British engineers who'd built the Chain Bridge. Near the tunnel, crowds were gathered to take the funicular railway the 95 meters up the hill to the Majestic *Buda Castle* and the *Fisherman's Bastion*, the neo-Gothic terrace built at the end of the 19th century in commemoration of the guild of fisherman who'd defended the castle during the middle ages. Looking up, O'Reilly could just see the soaring tower of the one-thousand year old *Mathias Church,* originally named the *Church of Our Lady* but popularly given the name of the 15th century conqueror of the Ottomans, King Mathias, the reformer who became Hungary's and all of Bohemia's great renaissance king. The taxi circled the roundabout in front of the tunnel then drove north, following the Danube, which O'Reilly, with a sense of irony, noted was muddy brown, rather than blue. When they reached the outskirts of a quaint village called *Szentendre*, the driver slowed. "A lot of Serbs live in this area," he said. "It is a quiet town, except for the tourists. Many people who visit Budapest come to *Szentendre* to see what an ancient Hungarian village looks like. But outside of the old town it is very quiet. I take you to an address. Serbs live there. I don't know why you want to go there." Jerzy was still playing it safe.

The road had been crowded, but O'Reilly had been able to glimpse Magetti's car amidst the traffic behind them on several occasions. When they pulled off the main road, he saw the black Mercedes cruise by. The house was down a narrow driveway and Magetti could not miss that the taxi had taken the road. They drove down the driveway to a lone two-story building that looked like a farm house. It had a stone foundation and cream-colored plaster walls and was covered by a rust-colored tile roof. Off to one side sat a wooden barn and another small outbuilding. The area in front of the house was gravel, and three cars were parked in front. The taxi came to a stop in front of the front porch. "This is it," the driver said.

"I'll pay you to wait," he told him.

"I don't like to sit here. Looks funny. You may be a long time." The man answered.

"I don't think I'll be more than an hour," O'Reilly told him.

"Call me. I will come back," the man answered. He turned the cab around and headed back out the long driveway.

Chapter 23

There was a screen on the front door and behind it the door was open. He opened the screen and walked inside. There was no mistaking the good-looking face of the man who came into view as soon as he entered the house. It was Dmitri Dragic.

Dragic was coming out the doorway of what looked as if it was a parlor at the end of a six-foot entrance hall. There were open doorways to either side of the hall. Dragic startled when he saw O'Reilly standing inside the front door directly in front of him. "What are you doing here? You're supposed to ring." Dragic was dressed in a cheap-looking suit and wore a dirty white shirt and a tie. His handsome mouth was turned down at the corners in a sneer. His chin jutted forward belligerently.

"The door was open," O'Reilly answered. "Are you in charge?"

Dragic scowled further. "No, I'm not in charge. If you'd rung the bell, Bratislav would have greeted you. He's in that room over there." He pointed to the open doorway on O'Reilly's left.

"Can you introduce me to him?" He didn't want Dragic to leave.

Dragic thought a moment, then nodded. "Sure. No problem." He motioned for O'Reilly to enter the open doorway.

The décor was nicer than that in the previous two brothels O'Reilly had visited that day. There was a long, faded red antique-looking sofa with a table and lamp at one end and three well-stuffed expensive-looking brocade chairs scattered about the room, each with a small table next to it. A dark-complexioned, middle-aged man sat in one of the chairs. He was dressed in a sleek blue suit and a white shirt and dark tie. Two rough-looking men, both of them dressed in slacks and open-necked shirts, were seated on the other two chairs. Each of them looked as if he weighed at least two-hundred pounds. They both had the bored look of employees. O'Reilly was unsure whether the well-dressed man also worked there until he stood up.

"What is this, Dmitri? A customer has come in without me knowing it?" The man had a smile on his face, but his tone carried a threat.

Icy fear shone in Dmitri's eyes. "He let himself in. I found him in the hallway."

"The door was open," O'Reilly said, looking straight at the man in the suit. "Anyway, I thought this was a business establishment."

The man turned to him and smiled, holding out his hand. "That it is. And you are welcome, no matter how you got in. My name is Bratislav Vucovic. You are here for entertainment, am I right? Mister…?"

"Smith," he answered. "You're absolutely right. I'm looking for entertainment." He still was keeping one eye on Dragic, who had gone over to the doorway and was leaning against the doorframe. "I heard you have girls from all over Europe here."

"Really?" the man said, his tone curious. "Where did you hear that?"

"A guy in a bar. He had a friend who had come here… or someplace like this. When I described the place to the cab driver, he brought me here."

The man nodded. Then he turned to the two men sitting in the other chairs. "Goran, Filip… get up and let our guest sit down. You two must have something to do. Go check on the girls and see who is awake." He turned back to O'Reilly. "Have a seat. Can I have Dmitri bring you something to drink? Whiskey? Beer? Wine?"

Keeping Dmitri occupied seemed like a good idea. "How about a glass of whiskey… with ice if you have it."

The man looked at Dragic, who nodded and left the room.

O'Reilly sat in the chair nearest Vucovic. "You really have girls from all over? How do you get them way out here in the countryside?"

Vucovic laughed. "It's easy. Girls like to work for us. We're a good employer, we keep our girls healthy, we pay them well. Everyone likes to work for Bratislav Vucovic." He laughed again.

Dragic returned with a glass of whiskey and handed it to O'Reilly, then looked to Vucovic for approval. Vucovic nodded.

"Do you have any Italian girls? Or if not, someone Polish?" O'Reilly asked, sipping on his drink. It was cold but it wasn't good whiskey. Whiskey wasn't usually his drink anyway.

Vucovic's face broke into a broad grin. "We can do better than that. We have a girl who is Polish but grew up in Italy. A very shy girl. I am sure that you'll like her."

The description fit Marina Stepovich to a T. If he could talk to her he could find out what had happened to Julietta. "How shy is she? I want her to do some special things."

"She will do whatever you ask… anything." Vucovic laughed.

"She sounds perfect. Can I see her?"

"Certainly. As soon as you finish your drink, Dmitri will take you upstairs to meet her. I am sure that you will be pleased."

"I am too," he answered. "How much will I be paying?"

"A girl like this is very special," the man answered. "We have had to pay for the expense of bringing her all the way from Italy. And you know those Italians… and the Polish too!" He laughed. "They eat like horses, even the small, delicate one's like this one."

"How much special?" O'Reilly asked.

The man smiled. "It really depends on how long you spend with her and what you want. She will tell us afterward and we will tell you the cost. Don't worry, it will be fair."

"Fair to whom? I'd rather know in advance."

"Ah yes. That would be good, but then we don't know what you want. Even if you tell me now, you may change your mind when you are with the girl. You have money with you? Credit cards?"

"I have five-hundred Euros and some credit cards."

The man smiled broadly. "Then why worry? You will get your money's worth. I guarantee it."

O'Reilly smiled back. He gulped down the rest of his drink. "Then take me to her."

Chapter 24

There was no sign of the other two men out in the hallway. As he followed him up the staircase to the second floor of the house, O'Reilly tried to judge whether Dmitri was armed. He remembered Benny at the first brothel… and Benny's gun. He couldn't see any gun on Dmitri, but who knew what he was concealing under his coat? And there were probably other guns on the premises, perhaps being carried by Vucovic or the other two men. He had the Glock that Sergio Magetti had given him tucked in the small of his back.

They walked down a hallway, past two closed doors, then stopped in front of a third door. Dmitri opened it without knocking. "You have a guest, Marina."

O'Reilly recognized Marina Stepovich from her photo, even though her face was red and puffy from crying and perhaps from a beating. When she looked up, fearfully, her eyes were glazed, as if she had been drugged.

"Marina speaks English, Italian and Polish," Dmitri said proudly. "She's a little shy, but don't let that worry you." He looked at Marina. "You'll be nice to the man, won't you honey? We don't want any trouble do we?"

Marina nodded dully and hung her head.

"If I need you to get her to cooperate, will you be around?" O'Reilly asked. He wanted to make sure that Dmitri didn't get too far away.

Dmitri chuckled. "Sure mister. Just call me. I'll be down at the end of the hall. Marina does whatever I tell her to do." He gave the frightened girl a meaningful look.

"Great," O'Reilly said, trying to look relieved.

"Have fun you two" Dmitri said, shutting the door behind him.

O'Reilly moved over to the door and listened to Dmitri's footsteps moving down the hallway, then he turned to Marina. She was sitting on the bed, her feet pulled up tightly against her, circling her knees with her arms. She stared at him with a frightened look.

He walked over to the bed and sat down near her feet. She pulled them up even closer to her body... away from him.

"Don't be afraid, Marina," he said in a low voice. He took out his Cruise Line ID card from his pocket and showed it to her. "I was sent by the *Adriatic Voyager*. We know that Dmitri kidnapped you. I talked to your parents in Naples. I'm going to get you out of here."

Her eyes widened. She began to cry. "You spoke to my parents? They know what happened to me?"

He shook his head. "They just know that you came to Budapest with Dmitri looking for a job and they haven't heard from you." He touched her on the shoulder. She startled at his touch. "I won't hurt you," he said. "I need to know if Dmitri brought someone else with you. "

143

She looked up at him. "He brought my friend. He tricked her." She began to cry.

"Don't cry, Marina. I'm going to get you out of here. But what happened to your friend?"

She looked at him with trusting eyes. "She is here. He brought her here. But they have beaten her many times. My friend is very strong-willed. She is rich and her father is a powerful man."

So Julietta was here! He needed to find her before he dealt with Dmitri. "Where is she?"

"Down the hall… in one of the rooms."

He thought for a moment, then realized he could use the same ruse he had used at the first brothel. He opened the door and called for Dmitri.

"She is giving you a hard time?" the young man asked, hurrying down the hallway. He had a superior grin on his face. "I can make her cooperate."

"No, no," O'Reilly said. "She's fine. But I want another girl too." He grinned back at Dmitri. "I like to double my pleasure. Marina says she has a friend who came here with her." He gave Dmitri a conspiratorial wink. "I think she may have an interest in the friend. I'd like to see how they do together."

The young man nodded as though he understood. "No problem. But you will pay more for two girls, you know." He looked up and down the hallway. "I can make you a special deal, mister. Give me a hundred Euros and I'll bring the girl and we don't need to tell them downstairs. It's a big

144

discount. Vucovic will charge you five hundred for her."

"So I give you the money and you won't tell Vucovic?"

"It'll just be between you and me," Dmitri said, a sly grin on his face.

O'Reilly pulled out his wallet and peeled off a hundred Euro note and handed it to the young man. "Get her."

In a few moments there was a knock on the door. O'Reilly opened it. Dmitri was standing in the hallway with a young, blonde woman, her head hanging as she twisted in Dmitri's grip. He shoved her at O'Reilly. "She is not so nice as Marina. I think you will have to show her who is boss."

As the girl stumbled through the door, Dmitri caught her by the hair, then reached around and grabbed her chin and made her raise her face. It was covered with bruises and brand-new red welts. "I have had to hit her to get her to come to you. I think you will need to hit her more."

O'Reilly wasn't listening. He was staring at the young woman, who stared back at him in defiance. She wasn't Julietta Martini.

He pulled the girl into the room and slammed the door on Dmitri. He turned to Marina. "Who is this?"

"It is Helena, my friend," Marina answered, looking at him in confusion.

"What about Julietta?"

Marina looked even more confused. The other young woman had gone over to the bed and

145

sat down, holding her head in her hands. She was sobbing.

"Julietta?" Marina asked. She looked as if she didn't understand.

"Julietta Martini… from the cruise ship. Dmitri brought her with you from Naples."

Marina still looked confused. She shook her head. "Dmitri did not bring Julietta here. He brought Helena and me."

"Your parents said that you and Dmitri went to look for Julietta after you left their house. Dmitri wanted to take her here with you."

She shook her head more vigorously. "We went to get Helena. She is my friend. She is rich, the daughter of a politician. Dmitri talked her into coming with us. She was just coming for the weekend, but he forced both of us to come here with him."

"And Julietta?"

"I never saw her again after we let her out of the taxi in downtown Naples."

"So Dmitri didn't kidnap her?"

She shook her head slowly. "Only me… and Helena. He kidnapped both of us." Her eyes were starting to look sleepy, as if the drugs were having an effect.

He shook her shoulder gently. "You have to stay awake, Marina. How many men are here in this house?"

She looked around, wide-eyed. "I think there are three or four. Dmitri and two big men who hit me and hit the other girls and gave us pills and shots. Another man is here sometimes… like a boss."

"Have you seen any guns?"

She looked even more frightened. "Guns? No… do they have guns?"

"I don't know." He looked around the room. "Is there a back way out of the house?"

"I think so, but it's downstairs."

That meant that he had to go down the stairs and into the main hallway. He was sure to run into someone. It was time to call in some reinforcements. He took out his cellphone and dialed Magetti. "I've found two girls. Neither of them is Julietta. Dragic is here, too. I'm taking the girls out, but I'm probably going to run into trouble. I need you to be ready to come in if I do."

"Forget the girls," Magetti said. "We want Dragic. He'll know where Julietta is."

"He didn't take her. He left her in Naples."

"Bullshit," Magetti exploded on the other end of the line. "He took her somewhere. If she's not there, then he knows where she is."

"There's three other men here besides Dragic. They're probably armed."

"Too bad for them. Do something to distract as many of them as you can, and hit the redial button on the phone when you want me to come in. That will be my signal. I've got men at the back of the house already, and I'll come through the front door."

"That's going to be either suicide or murder."

"It's not going to be suicide. Think of something to distract them and give me the signal." Magetti hung up.

"Christ," O'Reilly said. "This is going to be messy. Marina, Helena you have to do exactly as I say."

The blonde haired girl looked up. "Who are you? What do you want to do with us? Do you work for my father?"

"I work for the cruise line that Marina worked on. I know her parents. I'm going to get you out of here. But you have to do exactly as I say. There might be shooting."

Her face showed her fear, but also her defiance. "I will do whatever you tell me to do."

Chapter 25

O'Reilly moved to the door and called loudly for Dmitri. He heard the young man's footsteps coming back down the hallway. He took out his gun and stood to one side of the door.

The door opened and Dmitri marched into the room. "Need a little help with the girls, mister?"

O'Reilly closed the door with his foot and stuck the Glock into Dragic's back. "Keep your mouth closed Dmitri, or you'll be dead before the words get out of it." He motioned for Marina and Helena to come over beside him. "We're gonna walk downstairs, with you in front of us and then we're gonna walk through that front door." He took his cell phone out of his pocket and put his finger over speed dial, then he shoved the gun hard into Dragic's back. "Start walking."

"Who *are* you?" Dragic asked, not moving.

"If you don't start walking, I'm going to become your worst nightmare." O'Reilly prodded him in the back with his gun.

"They'll blow you away before you get out the door," Dragic said as they headed down the hallway.

"I told you to keep quiet. If they shoot anyone, it will probably be you. If they don't, I will."

They reached the top of the staircase. There was no one visible in the hallway below. O'Reilly pushed Dragic again, and the young man began

149

descending the stairs. He had started to shake. O'Reilly could see his shoulders heaving with big sobs. He had to hold the young man up with one hand to keep him from collapsing on the stairway. When they neared the bottom of the stairs, O'Reilly heard footsteps in the room off to the right—the one in which he'd met Vucovic and his two henchmen.

Just as they reached the bottom of the staircase, Vucovic stepped out of the room. He was smiling, but his smile immediately disappeared. "What is going on?"

"Dmitri, Helena and Marina are leaving… with me," O'Reilly said, flashing the Glock so Vucovic would make no mistake about him being armed.

Vucovic stared at him. "I don't understand. What is happening?"

"I told you we're leaving," O'Reilly answered. "Get out of our way."

"I'm afraid that's impossible," Vucovic answered, his face now serious. "Filip, Goran…" he half turned toward the room he had just left.

O'Reilly pressed the redial button on his cellphone. He heard it dialing. Then Filip and Goran were standing in the doorway to the room, both of them with guns in their hands.

"You see it is hopeless. I'd advise you to put down your gun. Poor Dmitri is not so valuable we wouldn't shoot him in order to stop you from leaving."

Before O'Reilly could answer, there were heavy footsteps coming down the hallway from the back of the house and at the same time the crash of footsteps on the front porch. The front door flew open and Magetti burst through it, gun in hand. Filip and Goran raised their guns to fire, but a burst of gunfire from behind O'Reilly blew one man's chest wide open and took off the top of the other's head. O'Reilly ducked and grabbed both Marina and Helena, pulling the two of them under his arm. In the confusion Vucovic reached inside of his coat. Magetti put a bullet through his neck, sending blood spurting as far as O'Reilly and the two women. Dragic had dived for the other doorway leading from the hall, but had landed short of it. He rolled over on his back and reached inside his coat. His hand emerged with a gun in it. He took a shaky aim at Magetti, who was standing over Vucovic's body.

O'Reilly fired, hitting Dragic in the shoulder and knocking him backward onto his back. His gun dropped to the floor, but, screaming in pain, he turned on his stomach, his gun within inches of his hand. Magetti's bullet caught him in the center of his back and he fell face-first on the floor, dead.

O'Reilly stared at the carnage in the hallway. Dragic, Vucovic and the latter's two employees were dead on the floor. There was blood everywhere. "What in the hell did you kill Dragic for?" O'Reilly demanded of Magetti.

The young Italian's face was flushed. His eyes were bright with excitement but there was also a look of horror on his face. "He was going for his gun. He would have tried to kill one of us. I had to shoot."

"I thought you wanted to question him about Julietta?"

Magetti's expression turned serious. "I did. He is the key to what happened to her. All these men were. But now they are all dead."

"Julietta's not here."

"But they no doubt took her," Magetti said, looking O'Reilly in the eyes.

"I don't think so. Marina said that Dragic never tried to take her from Naples. He took Marina off the ship and then grabbed her friend, Helena. That's all he took. No one else."

Magetti looked at Marina. She was huddled against O'Reilly, still shaking in fear. Her eyes were wide with fright. Helena was standing, the look of defiance still on her face as she stared back at Magetti "These girls only know what they saw," Magetti said. "Someone else from their group may have taken Julietta when Dragic couldn't find her."

"So where is she? Here?"

"There are other women here. We need to search."

"We need to get out of here before the neighbors call the police and we're all in jail for murder."

Magetti didn't look bothered. "We can take care of the police. I will call some people who can come and clean things up after we leave."

"Call some people? What the hell kind of people do you know who clean up dead bodies?"

"Mr. Martini has many contacts throughout Europe. They owe him favors."

O'Reilly just shook his head.

None of the other nine girls in the house was Julietta. O'Reilly wasn't surprised. Magetti didn't act surprised either, although he kept insisting that the group had kidnapped Julietta and that they were holding her somewhere. "It may not even be in Budapest," he said.

"You're crazy," O'Reilly told him. "I don't think she was kidnapped at all. I'm certainly not going to visit any more brothels looking for her."

"So you are ending your investigation?" Magetti asked. He looked hopeful.

"Curb your enthusiasm," O'Reilly answered. "I'm still going to look for her, but I'm not assuming she was kidnapped."

"There is no other explanation."

"There are lots of other explanations. We just don't know what they are."

"I will tell Mr. Martini that you are no longer working with me."

O'Reilly looked at him. Magetti was pigheaded. He had guts and his quick assault on the house had saved O'Reilly's and Marina's and Helena's lives, but he was stubborn and apparently dumb. O'Reilly had been suspicious about the idea of a kidnapping in the first place and now he was sure that that wasn't what was going on. But

Magetti had a one-track mind. And it was headed down the wrong track.

"Is one of those cars out there, Dmitri's?" he asked Marina. She looked out the front door and pointed to a battered green Opel. He wasn't about to call Jerzy and have him see what had happened in the farmhouse.

O'Reilly knelt down beside Dragic's body and felt in his pant's pocket. He pulled out a set of car keys. "I'm taking these two girls back to Naples," he said to anyone who was listening. With that he took each of the young women by the arm and walked out the door.

APPOINTMENT IN MYKONOS

Chapter 26

The *Adriatic Voyager* had arrived in Naples and was docked at the cruise ship terminal. Captain Firestone wasn't surprised to see O'Reilly back… but he was surprised when the detective refused to accept payment for his services.

"Julietta is still missing. I haven't finished what you hired me to do," O'Reilly told his friend.

"Magetti said that you found Dragic. He's sure that Julietta was kidnapped by the group Dragic worked for, but he hasn't found any leads yet. He's still in Budapest looking. He recommended that Martini pay you and send you home." They were back in the Officer's bar, both of them having drinks.

"Magetti shovels more bullshit than a streetcleaner in Pamplona. We found Dragic all right, and Magetti killed him before he could tell us anything. Dragic had kidnapped Marina Stepovich and one of her friends from Naples… the daughter of some rich politician. Marina said that Dmitri hadn't taken Julietta. Magetti refuses to believe it. Anyway, he wants me to go home, although I'm not sure why. On his own, the guy is about as adept as a one-armed paperhanger."

Firestone's face showed his puzzlement. "Why would he tell Martini to let you go, then? He was quite complimentary about your part in tracking down Dragic."

155

"Head-up-the-ass syndrome probably. Or professional jealousy, maybe. He couldn't stand being constantly shown up by a real detective."

"Even when his boss' daughter's life is at stake... someone he obviously is attached to? That's taking professional jealousy pretty far, don't you think?"

O'Reilly had been thinking the same thing. He shook his head. "Beats me. So what do I have to do to get rehired?"

"You still want to look for Julietta? Do you know something that Magetti doesn't know?"

"I know that she wasn't kidnapped by Dragic, nor, I suspect, by anyone. That means that she is missing because she wants to be missing."

Firestone looked even more perplexed. "Really? You mean you think she ran away?"

O'Reilly nodded. "That's what I think. Maybe she realized that with the crew on the ship knowing her, it was just a matter of time before her parents found out where she was. So she left the ship in Naples and disappeared."

Firestone let out a low whistle. "So she might still be in Italy."

"Why not? She told Anka that she had visited a lot of Italian cities, so she knows her way around the country. It makes more sense to go someplace you know than to try to hide in a strange land."

"Any clues?"

"Zip. I think I need to talk to her parents. They would know where she might go. Anyway, I need to talk to Alessandro Martini to get my job back. Can you arrange that for me?"

Firestone sighed. "Martini is difficult to deal with. You're going to be contradicting his most trusted security officer. You could just take the money you've earned so far and go home... or finish out the cruise and relax."

"I want to talk to Martini. Speaking of finishing the cruise, has my ex-wife's boyfriend beaten up any of your staff yet?"

"He's been a gentleman. I had dinner with him and Phyllis the second night out. I wouldn't call him pleasant, but he didn't eat his steak with his fingers or drink out of the water pitcher."

"How was Phyllis?"

"Trying to fit in with the upper classes, I'd say... or what she thinks are the upper classes. She wore more jewelry to dinner than Queen Elizabeth. But the boobs popping out of her dress gave her away."

"Once a trollop always a trollop," O'Reilly said.

"Sterling enjoyed it."

"The novelty wears off. Trust me," O'Reilly answered. He took a sip of his gin and tonic. "How long are you in Naples?"

"We leave first thing in the morning."

"So I could stay overnight and get off in the morning before you leave?"

"You could leave now if you want to. Martini lives in Venice. I'll call him this afternoon and tell him you're coming."

"Tomorrow will be fine. I'll need a room."

Firestone grinned. "Anka?"

"I need to thank her for her help. Anything less would be rude."

"And you've always been such a polite soul."

"I'm like Phyllis, I guess. I'm trying to take on the manners of my betters."

"Once a trollop always a trollop," Firestone said, chuckling and shaking his head.

Chapter 27

Despite his lack of a reservation he was able to use his cruise line ID card and a mention of his personal relationship with the ship's captain to secure a table in *Provence*, the ship's exclusive French restaurant. He had expected to be greeted by Anka, but the Maître d' was a young Filipino man, who smiled graciously and offered to seat him near a window. When he asked about Anka he was told that she was in the kitchen, supervising.

"Could you tell her that Brian O'Reilly is here?" he asked. "I'd like to speak to her."

When she appeared, Anka was dressed in an all-white dress; a ship's uniform, but short enough to reveal her shapely lower thighs, although unlike the blouse of her previous uniform, demurely buttoned nearly to her neck. Her always cheerful face was brightened by a wide grin and her green eyes sparkled with delight when she saw him. When he stood, she gave him a warm hug, which served to remind him of the softness of her ample breasts. She brushed her lips across his cheek.

"I thought I might not see you again," she said. There were tears in the corners of her eyes, although she could not rein in her ecstatic smile.

"I'm only here until morning," he answered. "You're not Maître d' any longer? Did fraternizing with me get you fired?"

He had pulled out a chair for her and they both sat.

"I've been promoted," she said, beaming with pride. "You brought me luck."

"So you are in the kitchen?"

"I'm the manager. I am in charge of both the kitchen and the dining room. We had a retirement in one of the other restaurants and they moved everyone about. The manager's position was available here in *Provence* and I applied and was accepted."

"Congratulations. You're on your way up the ladder."

She searched his eyes. "I hope so. Do you disapprove?"

"Not at all. I hope that doesn't mean your nights are never free."

"They're free for you. I'm off at eleven-thirty." Her expression became serious. "Did you find Julietta?"

He shook his head. "It's a long story. I'd like to tell you about it." He gave her what he hoped was a seductive smile. "Your cabin or mine?"

Her mouth broadened into a wide smile. "Mine. I got a cabin to myself as part of my promotion. And I stocked my bar with gin... just in case you came back."

"The girl of my dreams."

O'Reilly always kept his priorities straight. His reunion with Anka in bed took precedence over everything else. Afterwards, she fixed him a gin and tonic and poured herself a glass of ruby-red Spanish Tempranillo, and they sat in bed and talked.

"Dmitri is dead?" Anka's wide green eyes showed her shock. "And you shot him?" There was fear as well as shock in her voice.

"I only wounded him. Magetti killed him. He didn't need to… although in the heat of a gun battle, lots of people don't stop to think a lot about what they're doing. They just react. I guess Magetti just reacted."

"But you didn't kill him. Weren't you just reacting too?"

"I'm a professional. Of course Magetti is supposed to be one too."

She narrowed her eyes and looked at him. "You sound like you don't like him."

"I don't understand him. He's too eager to believe that Julietta was kidnapped."

"You don't think she was?"

"Marina was kidnapped. Marina fits the profile… a loner, shy, someone who would trust a scumbag like Dmitri because she's naïve. That's who kidnappers prey upon… all over the world. They don't go after the daughters of rich businessmen unless they are after ransom."

"But you said her rich friend was also kidnapped."

"That was strange. Apparently Dmitri had to bring two girls back to Naples for some reason."

Anka lay back, as if she were thinking. She sipped her drink. "I'm just glad that you got Marina back. She must have been terrified."

He nodded. "Anyone would have been. She held up better than most would have. I'm glad I could bring her back to her parents."

She snuggled up next to him. "My hero."

"Get used to it. I'm that kind of guy."

"I like that kind of guy," she said, snuggling even closer. Her shorter, rounded body fit nicely against his long, lean frame. She lay her head on his bicep. "I like heroes with muscles."

His face became serious. "I like being a hero but my job was to find Julietta, and I scored a big fat zero on that one."

She also became serious. She turned back to him and gazed up at his face. "So what do you think happened to her?"

He took a sip of his gin and tonic. "I think she's in hiding somewhere. Why, I don't know. She's old enough she could just live her life separately from her parents, if that's what's bothering her. She doesn't have to disappear to do that."

Anka looked pensive. "Maybe she does. Her father is very powerful. Maybe he won't give her any freedom."

He shook his head. "I don't know. She was off at school on her own. Her father seems to be more concerned about his business' reputation than about going all-out to find her. It seems to me she could have had a lot of independence. Her father doesn't appear to care much about her at all."

"I think there's a man involved."

He studied her face. She was staring at her wine glass, her brow knitted in thought. "Seriously… or is that just the giddy young woman in you talking?"

She hit him playfully on the arm. "I'm serious. She not only wasn't interested in Dmitri, she wasn't interested in anyone when she was onboard. There are a lot of hot guys among the crew and she was very beautiful. She didn't even look at them."

"Just like you now that you've got me?"

"Exactly!" she said, smiling sweetly.

"Maybe she prefers women."

She gave him a reproachful look. "I would have known, trust me."

"So you think she's run off with someone?"

"That's my guess. Someone her parents wouldn't approve of. Someone her father would use his power to get rid of if he found out about him. Her father may not care about her, but he cares about appearances."

"So who… a rock star? An African? An American, God forbid? A Protestant? Who do Italians think is unacceptable?"

She shrugged. "I'm not an Italian."

"That's why I have to talk to Martini himself… and to Julietta's mother. First I have to get hired back on the case then I need to find out where her parents think she might go and what hints, if any, they've had about her being interested in someone. That is if your theory is correct."

"It's just a guess."

"It makes more sense than anything I've been able to come up with."

She put down her glass and looked him in the face. "Good! It makes me happy to be able to help you out."

He gazed back at her perfect face, her wide mouth, half open in anticipation, her green eyes looking deeply into his. "Well you know what I really need help with?"

"What?" She sounded as if she was eager to do whatever he needed done.

"I need to get close to someone… tonight."

"Then our needs fit together perfectly!" she said and took his drink from his hand and put it on the night stand. Then she rolled over on top of him. "Is this close enough?"

"It's perfect."

APPOINTMENT IN MYKONOS

Chapter 28

The ferry pulled up to the pier below the town square of Amalfi, and Julietta Martini, her blonde hair hidden by a silk scarf and wearing a pair of dark sunglasses, stepped onto the dock. No one had recognized her on the ferry from Naples. But then why would they? She was traveling under a false name, and just as she had expected, her father had not allowed anything related to her disappearance to appear in the media. That showed her exactly how much he valued her compared to the prospect of bad publicity for his precious business.

If her ruse had been successful, Sergio Magetti and his men would be in Budapest searching for Dmitri Davidovic, that sleazy Serbian who had jumped ship in Naples and whom they would assume had taken her with him. She just hoped that Marina had been smart enough not to go with that dirtbag to Budapest, as he had been pleading with her to do when they were in the taxi. He'd wanted Julietta to go too—to keep Marina company, he'd said—but there was no way she was going to go anywhere with Dmitri.

She'd kept a low profile in Naples for a few days, figuring that it would take a while for anyone to notice that she was missing. But once they'd found out she was gone and Sergio's men began looking for her, she had to leave. Amalfi was someplace she felt safe, even though she knew that she couldn't stay there permanently. At some point someone would figure out that the Mediterranean village where she and her mother had fled from her father's possessive gaze years ago would be a likely place for her to seek refuge.

She walked through the *Piazza del Duomo*, the town square, with its ancient church dedicated to St. Andrew, and up the busy *Via Lorenzo d'Amalfi* toward the *Hotel Amalfi*. Despite the nearly shoulder to shoulder crowds of tourists, she felt lonely. She had never been away from everyone she knew for so long. She missed her mother. She missed her roommates in Florence. She missed Sergio's constant presence, even though his constant reporting on her activities, ordered by her father, had irked both of them. But they both knew that Sergio had had no choice. Her father was his employer and if Sergio wanted to keep his job, he had to follow her father's orders.

But most of all she missed having someone to spend her nights with. Not just anyone of course. She missed her lover.

But she would not have to wait long. He would join her soon. Their complicated charade would work, and her father would call off the search, thinking that she was either dead or gone forever, and they would be free at last!

Chapter 29

The face on the front page of the *Cronaca di Napoli* almost jumped out at him. It was a picture of the man from the *Adriatic Voyager's* private casino— the man in the tuxedo who had cheated at the roulette table. O'Reilly's Italian might have been limited, but it was sufficient for him to recognize the word *morto*—Italian for dead. He picked up the paper from the rack on the airport newsstand and took it to the clerk at the cash register.

"Excuse me," he said, using his most winning smile. "I don't read Italian. What does this article say about his man?"

The clerk, a petite and strikingly pretty young Neapolitan, with jet-black hair pulled back in a pert ponytail, looked up at him, a look of surprise on her face. She stared at him with a look of curious intrigue, as if she thought he might be making a pass at her… a pass she looked as if she would welcome. He responded by giving her another of his most ingratiating smiles and tapped the picture of the man in the newspaper with his forefinger. "I may have met this man. Does it say that he's dead?"

She sighed as though in resignation and looked down at the paper he had thrust at her across the counter. Her dark eyes moved rapidly back and forth as she scanned the article. "His name is Marcello Bertolini. It says that he is the son of a wealthy family from Rome, but that he was

167

known to be involved with drugs and gambling and was not in contact with his family. His body was found in a car on a street here in Naples"

"Does it say how he died?'

She no longer looked as though she were hoping that he would make a pass at her. Her knitted eyebrows and her frown showed her discomfort. "It says he was shot... shot in the head." She looked up at him suspiciously... and with more than a little fear. "He was a friend of yours?"

"Just someone I met. Who is investigating—the Naples police?"

"The *Carabinieri*. They think it may be a *Camorra* killing." The *Camorra* were the loosely affiliated clans of Southern Italy who controlled all of the crime of the region and most of the politicians. They were infamous for their control of the industrial waste disposal industry and responsible for dumping millions of tons of toxic waste in unshielded sites near population centers. The area northeast of Naples where much of the dumping occurred had been labeled by the British medical journal, *The Lancet*, as the *Triangle of Death* because of the high incidence of cancer-related deaths related to exposure to toxic waste created by the *Camorra*. The criminal network was reputed to use children to drive the trucks into the dumping sites because of the reluctance of truck drivers to risk exposure to the waste in their truckloads. As Sergio Magetti had told him, the *Camorra* were also involved in kidnapping and prostitution. But what would have been their interest in a small-time gambler such as Marcello Bertolini?

He nodded and thanked the girl, then paid for the paper and folded it and put it in his carry-on bag. They had called his flight.

The direct flight from Naples to Venice took only a little more than an hour. As soon as he got himself settled in his seat, he took out the newspaper, which he had removed from his bag in the overhead bin above him. He stared at the picture of the dead man. The police obviously did not know that the man had been a passenger on the *Adriatic Voyager*, although they would find out soon enough if they did even a routine search of his recent whereabouts. But he had probably disembarked in Toulon, just as O'Reilly had. There would be nothing to link his death with his recent voyage. Except O'Reilly knew better. The man had cheated Alessandro Martini. And he had paid the price.

He thought about Martini. Captain Firestone had made the interview appointment for him and the billionaire had agreed to meet him. Because O'Reilly wanted to talk to Mrs. Martini as well as her husband, the meeting was at the banker's home rather than at his office. Ted Firestone had warned him about dealing with Martini. Did Ted know about the man who had been killed for cheating in the ship's private casino? O'Reilly doubted it. But Firestone knew what kind of man Martini was. The Captain had warned O'Reilly to be careful.

He refolded the newspaper and let his thoughts drift to the previous night with Anka. Was he falling for the Bulgarian woman? She was fifteen years his junior—not an insurmountable difference in ages but a sizeable one. And she had a career on the cruise ship that was important to her. His career back in Los Angeles was foundering, and he could barely support himself. He'd already lost one wife because he couldn't provide the kind of lifestyle she desired.

What was he thinking? He could have a relationship with Anka without thinking of marriage or of taking her back to California with him. So what if her career was important to her? It was better than being with some mindless bimbo who had no idea what she wanted out of life. O'Reilly wasn't the kind of person who could help Anka move up the management ladder within the cruise line business, but so far she seemed to be doing alright on her own. Why not just enjoy what they had at the moment? That seemed fine with her, so there was no need for him to complicate things by worrying about the future.

The plane began its descent, and he returned to the problem of Alessandro Martini. What could O'Reilly say to him? Clearly, Sergio Magetti wanted the daughter's disappearance wrapped up—wanted to assume that Julietta had been kidnapped by an Eastern European prostitution ring and then ... what? Let Martini's contacts with the European police or with the underworld continue the search for her, and in the meantime try not to embarrass Martini in front of his criminal and business associates? The alternative was to give up on the search—throw the man's daughter to the wolves and forget about her. No father would do that would he?

He wondered what kind of a man Alessandro Martini was.

APPOINTMENT IN MYKONOS

Chapter 30

The water taxi from the airport motored into the choppy waters of the *Giudecca Canale*. He was the only passenger, which forced him to respond to the driver's constant chatter, much of it in Italian, which he didn't understand. When they were opposite *San Giorgio Maggiore Island*, home of the 500 year old *Church of San Giorgio* at the junction of the canal with the open ocean, they turned inward to the *San Zaccaria* docks, which sat on the *Riva degli Schiavoni*, the wide and crowded walkway that ran from the mouth of the *Canal Grande*, the Grand Canal, halfway to the end of the city island, ending at the *Arsenal*, the old shipyard.

The dock, which was packed with jostling water taxis and *vaporetti*, the large waterbuses, which served as public transportation in the city, was directly in front of the historic *Hotel Danieli*, the fourteenth century palace that had been a hotel since the early nineteenth century and was reputed to be one of the ten most beautiful hotels in the world. It was also only a short walk from *Piazza San Marco,* the famous St. Mark's Square.

His appointment with Alessandro Martini was not for another hour so he walked along the broad walkway that bordered the Canal, crossing one or two small, arched bridges, and finally the *Ponte della Paglia*, from which he could see, by gazing up the narrow canal beneath it, the famous enclosed *Ponte dei Sospiri*, or Bridge of Sighs, which connected the Doge's Palace and the building that had once been the prison in which the Doge, the ruler of the city, had tortured his most important political opponents, whose agonized cries had given the bridge its name. Then, bursting in front of him was the *Piazza San Marco*—St. Mark's Square.

He had only seen pictures of Venice and none of them had done justice to the sheer immensity of the square and the massive, ornate Basilica that gave it its name. He picked a table at the *Caffe Florian*, the eighteenth century coffee house which was more upscale than some of the other restaurants and then ordered a coffee from the waiter, who was dressed formally in black pants, a white shirt, black vest and tie and an apron around his waist. To his right, back in the direction of the Basilica stood the impressive, 300 feet tall, *Campanile*, or bell tower of St. Mark's, dating from the early sixteenth century, but rebuilt in the 1900's after it mysteriously collapsed in 1902.

He was not surprised to be served a tiny cup of thick espresso and he did his best to savor it in the European way, but he still longed for a full, twelve-ounce cup of Starbucks coffee, the kind he was used to drinking every morning in order to be able to cope with his day. How the Italians got by on such a tiny cup of coffee was beyond him.

As he gazed across the plaza, which was starting to fill with tourists, he was startled to see Sergio Magetti, himself having coffee at another restaurant, but quite definitely gazing back at him with a determined stare. Finishing his espresso, he crossed the plaza and sat down across from Magetti, who had continued to stare at him with a decided frown.

"Becoming a tourist?" Magetti asked, as O'Reilly signaled the waiter for a cup of coffee.

"I'm curious about other tourists who are supposed to be in Budapest doing their job," O'Reilly answered.

"I'm not a tourist," Magetti answered, glowering at O'Reilly. "I live here. I have to report to Mr. Martini once in a while and he lives here too."

"So he does," O'Reilly said. "Does he know how little you know about his daughter's whereabouts?"

Magetti reddened. "He knows everything. He knows that I'll eventually find his daughter and those who took her will pay, just as Dragic did."

"Eventually is a long time. You're barking up the wrong tree, and if you hadn't killed Dragic, you'd know it. Mr. Martini had better hedge his bet if he wants to increase the odds of finding his daughter."

"He will not hedge his bet, as you say, with you. You have been dismissed."

"That remains to be seen."

"What do you mean?"

"I'm Martini's best chance of getting his daughter back, and I'm planning to tell him that. I have an appointment with him this morning."

Magetti clenched his jaws. His anger showed in his eyes. "You dare to come to my city and talk to my employer?"

O'Reilly smiled. "You know Americans. We always think we're free to do whatever we want."

"This is not America," Magetti growled.

"You're right," O'Reilly said, looking at his watch. "It's Venice and I have an appointment with your boss." He stood up. "Since it's your country, consider me your guest and take care of my bill." He turned and headed for the street.

APPOINTMENT IN MYKONOS

Chapter 31

He crossed the *Piazza*, heading toward the clock tower on the other side of the square, with its two massive statues of shepherds standing at its top striking an enormous bell and, below that the winged lion, the symbol of Venice, perched over a gigantic circular clock, which had but a single hand, showing the 24 hours of the day in Roman Numerals. He passed through the two-story high archway beneath the clock and entered the *Merceria dell'Orologica*, the street that would lead to the Grand Canal and eventually to Martini's house. Although the *Merceria* itself was a wide shopping street, on either side were scores of tiny alley-like streets, leading in every direction, all of them, no matter their size, packed with tourists. Finally he reached the Grand Canal at the *Rialto*, the canal's busiest section where dozens of canal-side restaurants allowed tourists to sit and sip coffee while watching the gondolas and *vaporetti* pass beneath the *Ponte di Rialto*, the Rialto Bridge, the sixteenth century stone bridge that was the oldest bridge spanning the Grand Canal and was filled with shops at the top of its steep steps leading up the center of its great arch. On the other side of the bridge was the famous open-air Rialto market with its fruit and produce stands, its fresh fish on ice and its dangling chickens and legs of ham and beef. The supplier to many of the city's restaurants, the market also contained countless stands devoted to trinkets, the kind

176

valued by the city's tourists, such as the replicas of the iconic masks used in the annual *Carnevale di Venezia*. Once he crossed the bridge, he was only shouting distance from Alessandro Martini's residence. He looked back once or twice to see if Magetti was following him, but he was nowhere in sight.

Martini's residence fronted on a street so narrow that two people could barely pass one another. The door was of highly varnished dark wood set into the side of a building, which stretched up four stories and looked exactly like each of the buildings on either side of it. An elderly butler in full livery answered the door and offered him a chair in a marble-floored vestibule while he informed Mr. Martini that he had a guest. O'Reilly turned down the offer of a chair and instead paced up and down the entrance hallway. In a few moments the butler returned and led him up a winding marble staircase to the second floor, then down a hallway, which ran the length of the house and terminated at a large window which looked out on the magnificent Grand Canal, passing almost directly beneath it. Below him the porch and steps from the house descended to a long dock to which was tied an old-fashioned looking but obviously powerful wooden speedboat.

O'Reilly stared down at the busy canal, watching the mix of gondolas, water taxis and waterbuses heading up the canal toward the Rialto. People in power always made you wait, he thought. They were much more interested in establishing their superior position relative to their visitor than in making him or her feel welcome. Most of the LA lawyers he worked for did the same thing. Intimidation—irritation—indifference—those were the stages his reaction to such treatment had taken over the years, and he was now at the point that when it happened he was aware of what it said about the person he was about to meet, but otherwise, he no longer cared. At least he was able to see an interesting view of gondolas and powerboats. In the distance, the picturesque Rialto Bridge was teeming with tourists climbing the steps of its arch, high over the canal.

The door to the study opened and he was summoned by a young, bookish-looking man dressed in a well-pressed dark suit and a tie, into the inner sanctum of Alessandro Martini. The study was book-lined, although so far as O'Reilly was aware, Martini had no academic training beyond high school and perhaps not even that. A *bureau Mazarin* with delicate inlaid woods on the top and sides and elegantly carved legs served as Martini's desk, although its top was nearly clear of papers, except those neatly piled in two equally ornate in- and out-boxes, both half-full. Martini himself stood behind the desk and, as O'Reilly entered the room, stepped around to the front with his hand outstretched.

"Mr. O'Reilly," Martini said, his voice warm with enthusiasm. He was a short, slightly rotund man, dressed in dark slacks and a shirt, open at the collar, with his shirt sleeves rolled part way up.

Dark hair covered his thick forearms and was visible at the neck of his open shirt. His face was round, and his dark hair was mostly a fringe around a shiny bald head. He had bushy eyebrows and a rather large nose. His thick lips were parted in a broad smile, showing white, even teeth. "I am most happy to meet you. I have heard wonderful things from Sergio Magetti about your effort to find my daughter."

O'Reilly shook his hand.

Martini motioned for him to sit in one of the two leather armchairs in front of his desk, and he took the other. "Would you like a coffee?" he asked. He had a pleasant, expectant look on his face, as if the two of them were going to be discussing vacation or dinner plans, rather than the disappearance of his only child.

O'Reilly accepted the offer, despite his two earlier cups, and Martini motioned for the young man who had remained in waiting at the door, to fetch the coffee… or to fetch someone who would bring it.

"I'm sorry that I wasn't successful in finding your daughter," O'Reilly began.

"But you did find the man, Dragic, who took her. That was an extraordinary feat. Sergio is confident that he can take things from there and is still looking in Budapest."

A servant in a white jacket appeared with a wheeled tray on which was a pot of coffee, two cups and two saucers as well as cream and sugar and several small pastries. The young man who had summoned him, had reentered the room and resumed his place, standing, as if at attention, near the doorway.

O'Reilly waited until the servant poured the coffee and had left the room. After taking a sip of the coffee, he looked Martini in the eyes. "Your daughter is not in Budapest, and Dmitri Dragic did not kidnap her. In fact, I don't believe she was kidnapped at all. "

Martini smiled back politely. "Sergio said you would say such things. He, of course believes differently, and he is the Chief of my security services. I am afraid I have no choice but to believe him."

O'Reilly continued to stare back at him. "You do have a choice. You choose to believe Magetti, who hasn't got the chance of a snowball in hell of finding your daughter. I'm sure that he has given you years of valuable service in terms of security, but both his experience and his expertise in investigating something like your daughter's disappearance are quite limited. Mine, on the other hand, are quite extensive. You ought to believe me."

A brief look of irritation passed across Martini's face, immediately replaced by one of curiosity. "Believe you and not my Chief of Security?"

"Or believe nothing. Magetti doesn't know where your daughter is and I don't either. He is pursuing one line of investigation and I would like to pursue another. Given the importance of the outcome, I don't see why you would turn your back on either of our investigations."

Martini took a sip of his coffee before answering. When he looked up, his face continued to show his curiosity. "What do you think happened to my daughter?"

"She has run away. She is somewhere in hiding."

"Ran away from what? Hiding from whom?"

"From you."

Martini's face showed his shock. Then his expression turned to anger. "That is outrageous. You want me to hire you, and you dare to insult me?" He stared at his guest, his eyes smoldering with indignation.

O'Reilly stared back at him, unblinking. "Don't let your sensitivities get in the way of your judgment. If you want to find your daughter you'll hire me."

Martini swallowed hard to control his emotion, then resumed his serious expression. "What makes you think Julietta is running away from me?"

"It is only a guess, but your daughter told several crew members on the *Adriatic Voyager* that she did not get along with you. She was on the ship in the first place because she was trying, in her words, 'to take a break from school and my family.' I think wherever she is, she is continuing to do just that."

"My daughter and I have no problems with our relationship," Martini said, his voice stern, as if he were testifying in court, although O'Reilly could hear the defensiveness in his tone. "She is nearly an adult. She lives on her own in Florence where she studies at the university, and she can do as she pleases without my permission. Why would she need to run away to gain her freedom?"

"That's a very good question," O'Reilly answered. "Someone suggested that perhaps your daughter has a boyfriend… someone of whom you wouldn't approve. Perhaps she has run off with him."

Martini looked even angrier. "That's preposterous. Sergio would have known if she was seeing a young man. He would have told me if she had a boyfriend. "

O'Reilly tried to conceal a smile. "If Magetti knew everything that your daughter was doing then her freedom was not so complete as you describe it."

Martini had reined in his anger but his expression was still extremely serious. "That is Sergio's job. My daughter is more valuable to me than anything. Of course I use my security services to keep an eye on her. Sergio has been doing that since she was a young child."

"So he told me. But he did a piss-poor job this time. She was gone several days before he was even aware of it."

"That was an unfortunate error. But since then, Sergio has done everything within his power to locate Julietta."

"You mean everything short of informing the authorities of her disappearance."

Martini's face reddened beneath his dark complexion. "Undue publicity would not serve anyone. I can't have the world thinking that I can't even protect my own daughter on one of my own cruise ships. My security services are just as capable as the police are of finding Julietta."

"That remains to be seen." He continued to look Martini directly in the eyes. "But since you are determined to keep the investigation discreet, then why not let me search for her too? Surely the money is no problem for you, and pursuing two leads is infinitely more productive than pursuing just one."

Martini looked away. He picked up his cup and sipped from it, distractedly. "You really think you might be able to find her?"

O'Reilly nodded. "I guarantee it. But I need to talk to your wife as well as to you. I need to know where your daughter's favorite places to go would be...places where she might feel safe. I also need your permission to search her room at the University of Florence and to talk to some of her friends there."

Martini looked alarmed. "The university does not know that she is missing."

"And they don't need to. But when I talked to the crew on the *Adriatic Voyager*—something which Magetti failed to do, by the way—I found that Julietta had confided in several of them. If she felt that free to talk to new acquaintances, then I'm sure that she confided in some of her friends at school."

Martini nodded slowly, his expression indicating that he was agreeing in spite of himself. "I suppose that makes sense. As for me, I have to confess that I don't know where Julietta liked to go or where she felt safe. We… we didn't actually talk very much. She confided in her mother more than in me." He looked somewhat sheepish. "I'm sure that that is normal for young women and their fathers."

O'Reilly didn't respond to Martini's admission. "Are you hiring me, then?" he asked.

Martini nodded. He turned toward the young man who had continued to stand next to the door. "Benito, give Mr. O'Reilly some cash and arrange for him to receive a credit card from Seven Seas Cruise Operations. Then take him to see Mrs. Martini." He stood up and held out his hand. "I wish you luck, Mr. O'Reilly. Benito—Mr. Buscaglia—is my personal secretary and he can arrange whatever you need. He will take you to my wife." He shook O'Reilly's hand and then turned and walked back around his desk, sat down and began reading one of the papers from his inbox.

Benito walked over and held out a hand toward the door. "Please come with me, Mr. O'Reilly. I will arrange everything you need."

APPOINTMENT IN MYKONOS

Chapter 32

Benito led him up the winding stairs of the four-story house until, on reaching the third floor, he halted, then turned and entered a long hallway which took two sharp turns before they arrived at their apparent destination in front of a closed door. The young man knocked softly. A female voice from behind the door inquired who was there.

"Benito, ma'am. I have Mr. O'Reilly to see you." He waited with a bowed head.

"Come in, Benito," the woman answered.

Benito turned the handle and opened the door, then ushered O'Reilly into the room ahead of him. They did not enter a bedroom, as O'Reilly had imagined, but a sitting room with several plump, well-cushioned chairs, upholstered variously in pale blue or a shiny aqua fabric, a dark blue loveseat done in some sort of fuzzy material and a writing desk with a leather chair in front of it. Mrs. Martini sat in a Queen Anne chair and was drinking coffee from a service, which sat on a low table next to her chair. Behind her was a large floor-to-ceiling window, its curtains open and through which could be seen the tops of the buildings lining the opposite side of the Grand Canal. She gazed at her two guests with a look of apprehension. When Benito approached, she did not stand, but kept her eyes glued to him, except for an occasional, furtive glance at O'Reilly, who stood back, waiting to be introduced.

"Good day, ma'am," Benito greeted the woman. His manner was deferent and gentle. "This is Mr. O'Reilly, who has been searching for your daughter. He has some questions he wishes to ask you."

She managed a brief, weak smile at the secretary, then turned her face toward O'Reilly. She was a beautiful woman, with striking cheekbones, made more prominent by her almost anorexic figure. O'Reilly was unsure if her thinness reflected an illness or was her usual state, since he knew she had been a model when she was younger. She had pale skin, having been born an Italian but with mixed German blood. Her eyes were enormous and were heavily shadowed by eye makeup. She had a long, straight nose and a rather narrow mouth, her lips painted with dark, ruby lipstick. Her hair was bright blonde and appeared to be natural. It was pulled back severely from her face so that it hung in a long cascade down her back. She was wearing a long-sleeved, black and white striped shirt, scooped at the neck to reveal her prominent collarbones, and a pair of loose black slacks. On her feet she wore a pair of shiny black sandals. The long slender fingers of both hands were adorned with rings, mostly diamonds.

She searched O'Reilly's face, as if looking for a clue as to whether or not he presented a threat. After a few moments, she nodded, then spoke. "Please take a seat, Mr. O'Reilly." She motioned toward another Queen Anne chair on the opposite side of the table. "Thank you, Benito. Will you please have some fresh coffee sent up? And a cup for Mr. O'Reilly." In contrast to her appearance, her voice was authoritative, though soft and pleasant, almost musical.

Benito, nodded and backed out of the room, much as if he were exiting the presence of nobility.

"You have spoken to my husband, already," she said gazing curiously at O'Reilly. "That he has allowed you to see me suggests that he has hired you to continue looking for Julietta."

"Yes he has."

"So Sergio will be coming back home? He is no longer continuing his search?" She looked concerned.

"Sergio and I will each carry out our respective investigations. I believe that he will continue to look for your daughter in Budapest."

Her face showed her relief. "I have great faith in Sergio. He cares deeply for Julietta. I am sure that he will find her. And you... where will you carry out your investigation?"

"That is what I am here to discuss with you."

She raised her eyebrows. "With me?"

"I don't believe your daughter has been kidnapped. I believe she is hiding somewhere. I wondered if you know the places where she would feel most safe... but also well-hidden." He found himself speaking quietly and gently, as if sensing that his interlocutor was fragile.

She was startled by his comment. "But Sergio was certain that Julietta has been kidnapped. Has he changed his mind?"

He shook his head. "No. Sergio still believes that your daughter was kidnapped. He is following up on that lead. I disagree with him and will look elsewhere."

There was a knock on the door. When Mrs. Martini bade the person enter, the same servant who had served coffee to her husband entered the room, pushing a serving table on rollers with a pot of coffee and two cups. He exchanged the service on the table for the new one and poured each of them a cup then left the room.

"Your daughter boarded the *Adriatic Voyager* because she was running away. She told several of the crew exactly that. She left the ship abruptly in Naples, without taking her belongings with her, making it look as though she had been kidnapped. In fact, another young woman left with her and even shared a taxi with her and was kidnapped by someone who had been posing as a crew member. This other girl and a friend of hers were taken to Budapest and made prisoner by a prostitution ring. Sergio and I rescued the other young woman and her friend and the man who took her was killed. The young woman said that your daughter was not taken by her captors, but Sergio does not believe that, whereas I do."

Mrs. Martini's face showed her concern, but she continued to gaze at him attentively. O'Reilly's methodical manner was keeping her anxiety under control. "What do you think did happen to Julietta?"

"I think she wanted to give the impression that she was taken but she actually fled somewhere. I am not sure why. She told the crew that she didn't get along with your husband, but I'm not really sure if that is sufficient reason to disappear."

"She is afraid of my husband. She was hurt by him when she was younger."

"Your husband told me that he had a good relationship with her."

She permitted herself a bitter laugh. "They have never been close. My husband is a warped individual. That is why I requested a bodyguard when Julietta entered puberty... to protect her from my husband."

"You mean Magetti? Sergio was protecting her from her own father?"

"Alessandro did not know that, but Sergio did. I requested a bodyguard and I took Sergio into my confidence. He knew that Alessandro had behaved inappropriately toward Julietta when she was younger. He made sure that the situation could not occur again."

"And your husband allowed that?"

She smiled. "Sergio and I concocted various stories that would make it seem as if Julietta and I needed his constant presence. Of course, when Julietta became an adult at 18 and left for university, that was no longer necessary."

"But she felt it was necessary to run away... even after leaving for the university."

"That is what you say. Sergio does not think so. I know that Julietta's safety is Sergio's first concern. I trust his opinion."

"I don't doubt Sergio's concern for your daughter. But I am trained to find people, and I have a different opinion. Someone suggested that your daughter might have a boyfriend... perhaps someone whom your husband would not approve of. Perhaps she ran away to be with him."

Mrs. Martini looked thoughtful. "I suppose that could be true. Alessandro would be very particular about whomever Julietta saw. He might even harm someone who was with her whom he didn't approve of. My husband is very possessive. Julietta does not want to end up becoming his prisoner as I have." She uttered the words without emotion.

"You mean you are not free to go when and where you wish?"

"My husband has Sergio's men report to him about everything I do. I rarely leave the house any more. I am afraid I am being kept much like a prize bird in a cage."

"And he behaved similarly toward Julietta?"

"Yes, but she was not so docile as I. They continued to have conflicts up to the point that she left for university. He wanted her to go to the local university so she could live at home, but she refused."

"Your husband said that Sergio would have known if she was seeing someone—a boyfriend."

She sipped her coffee before answering. "Sergio knew most of what Julietta was doing, but as she got older, she wanted to be left alone. She could have gone behind his back. Sergio was a good bodyguard, but he was very trusting of Julietta. She could have easily fooled him if she wanted to."

"So that gets back to my earlier question. Where would your daughter go? Where would she feel safe from your husband but also be in someplace that was familiar to her?"

She smiled, as if recalling a pleasant memory. "That is easy… Amalfi. She and I visited there once without telling Alessandro where we were going." She blushed and lowered her head. "We needed to get away from him. We told him we were going somewhere else. Sergio knew where we were. He visited us every other day, but he also sent false reports to Alessandro from Naples, where we had said we were staying."

"You stayed in a hotel in Amalfi?"

"Yes."

"And your husband never found out?"

"No. If he had known, he would have punished me and fired Sergio."

"Punished you?"

"My husband can be very cruel."

His curiosity urged him to ask what she meant, but it would serve no purpose to inquire further into the Martini's domestic habits. He knew full well the depth of Martini's cruelty because he had read about its consequences in the obituary of

Marcello Bertolini, the murdered gambler from the cruise ship.

"What was the name of the hotel in Amalfi?"

"The *Hotel Amalfi*. Do you really think that Julietta may be there?"

"It's a long shot, but it's possible. If she has a boyfriend, she might not be alone."

"You will go there?"

"After I stop in Florence and talk to some of her college friends. Do you have any of their names and can you call them to give them permission to talk to me?"

"I know one or two. I will write them down for you. I will give them a call." Her look of apprehension had returned. "If you find her you will have to tell Alessandro, won't you?"

"Your husband hired me. Do you think it would be dangerous for me to tell him?"

"I fear for Julietta and, if there is a young man involved, for him."

He looked her in the eyes. "My job is to insure the safety of your daughter. I will do everything in my power to do that, Mrs. Martini."

She returned his gaze, then reached out and grasped his hand tightly. "Please call me Sophia. I believe you, Mr. O'Reilly. I hope you find Julietta. I trust Sergio completely, but I would much rather that my daughter has run away and is safe and in hiding than that she has been kidnapped by a gang who has forced her into prostitution, so I hope that Sergio is wrong and you are right."

APPOINTMENT IN MYKONOS

"So do I."

APPOINTMENT IN MYKONOS

Chapter 33

On either side of the highway leading from the airport toward Florence, rolling hills spread toward the horizon. Every hilltop seemed to be crowned with a large villa, most of them with a second or third building, presumably housing the equipment needed to farm the extensive olive orchards and vineyards which flowed down the hillsides. Finally the city was revealed ahead of him, a hodgepodge of white, pink and brown buildings, sprinkled with church domes and bell towers, cut in two by the pale green Arno river meandering through is center. In the distance he could make out the distinctive *Ponte Vecchio*, the medieval bridge populated by shops and apartments which rose two or more stories high from one end to the other as it spanned the wide river. He followed the *Viale Niccolo Machiaveli*, the tree-lined avenue that wound along the wooded hillsides above the river and past the ancient villas of the city's forefathers, some of them now turned into hotels but many of them still the homes of the rich merchants of the town, then crossed the Arno after which he turned off and entered the imposing *Porta Romana*, the massive gate to the old city, still attached to a section of the wall which once surrounded what was now known as old Florence—or *Firenze*, as it was called, locally. Along a narrow street he parked his car. The streets were clogged with tourists, and walking was the only reasonable way to move about.

APPOINTMENT IN MYKONOS

The buildings of the university were spread throughout the city. *The Faculty of Literature* occupied a group of structures, dating to the 1600's, near the university administration buildings and only a few blocks from the *Galleria dell'Accademia*, the home of Michelangelo's *David* and the principal destination of the thousands of visitors who came to the city each day. O'Brien hoped to avoid the crowds, which lined up for blocks to enter the *Galleria* for a glimpse of the renaissance sculptor's masterpiece.

He entered a plaza, which was crowned by an immense white and green marble cathedral, which he learned from a sign was called *Saint Croce*, as was the plaza in front of it, the *Piazza San Croce*. The church, which was constructed over a period of 150 years and completed in the mid 15th century, was the final resting place for such illustrious residents of the city as Michelangelo, Machiavelli and Galileo, even Marconi, the inventor of the telegraph, as well as enough other luminaries to be nicknamed *Tempio dell'Itale Glorie*, the Temple of Italian Glories. In front of it stood an enormous sculpture of Dante Alighieri. In the distance he could see the *Duomo*, the rounded top of the 13th century *Basilica di Santa Maria del Fiore* that loomed above the rooftops of Florence and next to it, nearly as tall, the slender bell tower of *Giotto's Campanile*, which along with the octagonal *Battistero di San Giovanni*, or Baptistry of St. John, made up the three buildings of the *Piazza del Duomo* in the heart of the old city. Beyond that would be the administration buildings of the University of

Florence and nearby the buildings of the *Faculty of Literature*. Julietta had lived in an apartment nearby with two roommates, using the name of Sylvia Marconi, just another young student, nothing to identify her as the daughter of one of the richest men in Italy.

He made his way through the narrow, crowded streets toward the address Julietta's mother had given him. He had the names of the two roommates, who, thanks to Sophia Martini, were expecting him. The building itself stood out in no particular way from those on either side of it, and most of the pedestrians on the sidewalks were young people, probably students. Near the entrance was a café, with tables lining the sidewalk. Students sat drinking coffee and talking or reading. Up until a little more than a week ago Julietta Martini might have been one of these students sitting at a table having coffee with her friends… or with a boyfriend? O'Reilly hoped to have his questions answered.

He pressed the bell, and in response to the inquiry over the intercom, announced himself. He pushed open the door. Ahead was a winding staircase leading to the upper floors. Julietta's apartment was on the third floor.

The door was opened by a tall, dark-haired beauty, her black hair curling around her olive-complexioned oval face in long, graceful waves. Her large brown eyes widened as she took in O'Reilly, standing expectantly at the door.

"Mr. O'Reilly?" the young woman asked, a soft smile creasing her face.

He nodded and returned her smile.

"Maria and I have been waiting for you, please come in." She opened the door wide and stepped aside. "I am Christina Magnani."

"Brian O'Reilly," he said, extending his hand.

Her hand was soft and cool.

The apartment was sparsely furnished, although the chairs, the sofa and the coffee table looked elegant and expensive. Maria, the other young woman had risen and was standing in front of the couch. She was a shorter, somewhat plump girl with black hair and a dark round face, her eyes looking out with warm friendliness. She was no beauty such as her roommate, but she exuded an open aura that made O'Reilly feel welcome.

He took a seat in one of the leather chairs, and the two young women immediately sat on the couch in front of him. They looked at him expectantly. The taller woman, Christina's, gaze betrayed the attraction to him which had flashed in her eyes when she had first met him at the door, but O'Reilly found himself surprised by his lack of response. Christina was a beautiful young woman, but despite his awareness of her beauty, he felt a strong surge of allegiance to Anka, which left him stunned. Was this what it felt like to be in love? He tried to put such thoughts out of his mind.

"Would you like a coffee?" Maria asked, her mouth bowed in a sweet smile.

"That would be fine," he answered, relieved to be able to focus on what was going on in the room.

Maria slid back off the couch and went into the kitchen. Christina, the taller one, continued to gaze at O'Reilly. Her expression had turned to one of concern. "We didn't know that Sylvia—that's how we knew her until her mother called us—was missing. She said she was taking a break for a week and was going on a cruise." Her voice was low and sensuous, as if she were sharing an intimacy with him.

He ignored the invitation he sensed in her voice. "I'm not sure if I'd say she's missing," he answered, "so much as she may not want anyone to know where she is. She seems to have gone somewhere to be alone—or at least away from her parents."

Christina nodded. She hadn't shown any surprise at his words. "She did not like her father. She spoke of him with great anger. He had her watched, did you know?"

He assumed that she was speaking of Sergio Magetti. "I didn't know she was aware of that."

"It was no secret. Sergio, as she called him, talked to her regularly. She had him to the apartment once or twice. He was embarrassed to be spying on her."

It sounded as if Magetti even did his bodyguarding ineptly. "He said that or did she?"

"She told us. He was very polite when he was here, even though she tried to get him to relax.

She didn't seem to treat him as if he was an employee except to acknowledge that he had to know where she was at all times. She said neither of them liked that, but it was his job."

It had been clear from Magetti's behavior that he was more than a bodyguard and that he cared deeply for his charge. It only surprised O'Reilly to hear that Julietta apparently reciprocated his feelings and treated him more as a friend than as an employee. O'Reilly assumed that her acceptance of Magetti and his duties had given the security guard a false sense of confidence that he could trust her. She had manipulated his trust and used it to disappear.

Maria returned with a tray holding three cups of coffee. She set it down on a coffee table between them and gestured for O'Reilly to drink. The coffee was hot and strong.

"Was Julietta…I mean Sylvia, seeing anyone?" O'Reilly asked. "Did she have a boyfriend?"

The two girls glanced at each other. Maria looked embarrassed, as if she was being asked to divulge a confidence, but Christina looked back at O'Reilly with a steady gaze. "She never told us directly, but she met someone now and then and talked to him on the telephone at night."

"Met someone? Do you know where?"

Both women shook their heads.

"She stayed out all night several times." Christina said, still looking steadily at O'Reilly. Her eyes conveyed her trust in him, although she had not completely lost the indications of attraction that had been their since they first met. "I think she stayed with him, but she never talked about it and we didn't ask. We are all roommates, but things still stay private among us." She gave him a meaningful stare.

Despite being flattered that his charm still seemed to work, O'Reilly avoided returning her stare.

"We don't even know for sure that it was a boyfriend," Maria added, still looking embarrassed.

Christina turned to toward her. "It was a boyfriend, Maria. We both were sure of that." She turned back to O'Reilly. "But she never admitted it to us."

"And you didn't ask?"

"Sylvia was a private person," Christina answered. "She was very sweet and very considerate. We knew her father was rich, even though she tried to keep it a secret from everyone at the university, but she told us. She never acted high and mighty or as if she was better than us. She never showed off her money. But she kept to herself. She studied a lot. She loved to write and wanted to become a writer. But she had no friends except the two of us... and Sergio, who was watching her. And she hardly ever talked about herself."

"Except you knew how she felt about her father."

"She could not keep it inside of her."

"She was very bitter," Maria chimed in. "Her father was a tyrant with both her and her mother."

"Her mother said Sylvia had a favorite place to go, that her father didn't know about."

"Amalfi," both young women said at once.

"Yes."

"She talked about it," Christina said.

"She and her mother hid from her father there," Maria added.

"She told you a lot," O'Reilly said. "Did she give any hints that she wanted to go to Amalfi again?"

"Sergio knew about it. She wouldn't go there if she was trying to hide," Christina said. "That would be the first place he would look, I'd think."

O'Reilly agreed, but that hadn't been where Magetti had looked. The security guard's certainty about Julietta having been kidnapped had blinded him to the obvious.

"Or Mykonos," Maria said.

"Mykonos?" He knew that was the name of a Greek Island, but that was about all he knew.

The plump young woman looked self-conscious to have said anything, but she looked straight at O'Reilly and took a deep breath. "She told me once that if she ever wanted to get away from everyone she'd go to Mykonos. She'd been there before and she knew an old woman there whom she was very close to."

"A relative?"

Maria shrugged. "I don't know. She just said she knew someone there who was like a mother to her, but of course it wasn't her mother."

And her mother had never mentioned Mykonos, O'Reilly thought. Was that on purpose or did her mother not know how her daughter felt about the Greek island? At any rate he now had a second destination if Julietta was not in Amalfi.

"Do you mind if I have a look at Julietta's room?" he asked. He didn't expect to find any real clues to her disappearance, but it would be derelict of him not to search her belongings just in case. She might have left a calendar or a diary with the boyfriend's name or some such thing.

"Her mother told us to let you do whatever you needed to do," Christina answered. "You can stay as long as you like."

"I just need to see if I can find anything that would tell me where she went," he answered, ignoring the invitation that he heard once again in the beautiful young woman's voice. He was shown to Julietta's bedroom. Like the rest of the apartment, it was sparsely furnished but the bed and furniture were old and expensive. She had a small writing desk, but there was no calendar and the drawers, which were unlocked, contained no personal letters or diary. He guessed that she had removed anything that might provide information as to where she was going.

Her closet was only partially full, meaning that she had taken at least enough items of clothing for a short trip and maybe for a longer one. He searched through the pockets of her coats and jackets, hoping, without success, to find a scrap of paper or anything that might add to what he already knew. He left the bedroom empty-handed.

He thanked the two women for their cooperation.

Christina looked disappointed that he was leaving. "You are welcome to stay for lunch," she offered, her mouth parted in a sensual half-smile.

He knew he'd better leave before even his allegiance to Anka wouldn't be enough to overcome such a directly sexual bid for his attention from such a beautiful young woman. "I'm afraid I have to go."

"I hope that Sylvia is safe," Maria told him as he stood in the doorway.

"I think she is safe, but doesn't want to be found," he answered. Then he admonished them that her disappearance was a fact the family wanted kept secret from the university community. "And in case she is in any danger, it's important that she or whomever she is with not know that anyone is trying to track her down," he added. He knew that she would know that she was being searched for, but he wanted to impress upon the two young women the need for silence about Julietta being missing.

They both nodded.

Christina began to pout.

He thanked them again and said goodbye.

Chapter 34

To get to Amalfi he had had to return to the airport in Florence and then fly to Naples. From the airport in Naples he had rented a car for the trip to Amalfi. The drive from Naples to Sorrento in his rented MINI Cooper had been uneventful, other than his tendency to be distracted by the looming presence of Mount Vesuvius just inland from the highway. Like everyone who viewed the dormant, but not extinct volcano, he couldn't help but muse about the fate of the poor residents of Pompeii and Herculaneum, two millennia before. The foothills below the mountain were the site of scores of recently built housing developments, populated by thousands of Neapolitan suburbanites who were apparently unafraid of living in the shadow of a volcano which could become active again at a moment's notice. Perhaps their villages would someday become the archaeological wonders of some future civilization, which would muse, as he was doing now, on the plight of the poor devils who had ignored the warnings of history and science to tempt fate.

He had been warned that he himself was tempting fate by driving the dramatic and treacherous narrow mountain road from Sorrento to Amalfi, known as the *Amalfi Drive*. The rental car dealer had advised him that it was much safer to turn off the highway ahead of Sorrento and cross the peninsula from Pompeii to Salerno and take the half-hour ferry ride from there to Amalfi. O'Reilly was never one to choose an option just because it was safer. Besides, he had heard about the beauty of Sorrento, the coastal city which had existed all the way back to the time of the Greeks and was now a major tourist attraction, not for its history so much as for its scenery, and he wasn't about to miss the spectacular views from the cliffs that had made the city famous.

The views were everything they'd been cracked up to be. Sorrento was perched high above the sea, the waves of which crashed far below against the bases of the soaring cliffs on which the city was built. The more daring of the hotels had built stairways or elevators to the foot of the cliffs and constructed floating docks, which jutted hundreds of feet into the sea and were lined with beach lounges, umbrellas and seaside bars, to allow their guests to enjoy the water. The city park itself included two public elevators to the beaches below, but O'Reilly declined to take either, since he was only stopping for lunch, not planning to become a genuine tourist. He had gazed over the railings from atop the cliffs then walked the cobblestone streets of the old town before settling down at the café whose tables lined the edge of the main town square. It was time for a substantial meal and a stiff drink before attempting the hazardous road that led ahead.

The local swordfish steak was more than an ample lunch, followed by the town's signature lemon cake, all of which he washed down with a gin and tonic, although the waiter tried his best to persuade him to buy a bottle of white wine to go with his meal. He was tempted to sample the *limoncello*, the *digestif* made from lemon rinds, alcohol and sugar for which the town was famous, but one G & T was all the alcohol he could afford to drink before embarking on the challenging drive ahead of him.

The first leg of the highway was perfectly tame as O'Reilly headed inland from Sorrento and into the hills above the town. In contrast to his expectation, the road was relatively straight. Because of that, he was surprised that the tan SUV which was behind him didn't make any attempt to pass. He finally decided that the driver must be a non-Italian, like himself, since while he and the SUV crawled their way into the mountains, a handful of cars and a half-dozen motorcycles, all driven by what he assumed were crazy Italian drivers, zipped by him.

By the time he reached the coastal road, which hugged the sides of the cliffs high above the ocean, he had come to a more ominous conclusion regarding the tan SUV. He was being followed. Whoever it was, was making no effort to conceal the fact. The driver remained a steady three car lengths behind him. When he slowed, the SUV slowed. When he accelerated, the SUV kept up the same pace. O'Reilly was tempted to stop and force the man to either stop with him or pass. But there were almost no turnoffs and those that he happened upon, which were usually at vistas where tourists could take pictures of the magnificent scenery, were completely filled with other cars.

As the road settled into a series of tight curves it also narrowed. O'Reilly's outside lane ran perilously close to the small guardrail, which was all that stood between his car and a 300 hundred foot drop to the sea. As the SUV pulled closer, O'Reilly could see that there were at least two occupants in the car. When he came to a short straight section of the road, he sped up. The SUV also increased its speed and when he reached the next curve, which was a hairpin left, following the lines of a wide crevice in the cliff, the SUV was almost on his rear bumper. It began to inch closer. Instead of panicking, he became angry… angry at himself as much as the men in the SUV. How could he, driving a tiny, sleek, MINI Cooper and with years of police training in pursuit driving under his belt, allow an ungainly tub like the tan SUV to push him around on a road like this? He had visions of the chase scenes from *The Italian Job*, with MINI Coopers weaving in and out through shadowy storm drains and up and down the steep sides of the concrete LA Riverbed. Was he really going to let Jason Statham, Mark Wahlberg and Charlize Theron outdrive him?

Heading into the curve he took his foot off the brake and floored the gas pedal. The MINI Cooper leapt forward, screeching its tires as he held it to the curve of the road. Immediately ahead, the road turned abruptly back toward the sea. O'Reilly kept his foot on the gas and squealed around the next corner, the edge of the road rushing at him like the open jaws of a sea monster waiting to devour his tiny car. He waited as long as he dared, then stomped his foot on the brake, throwing him forward into his seat belt as the car decelerated and then, the moment that he cleared the apex of the curve, he was on the gas pedal again, accelerating toward the next corner. He glanced in his rear-view mirror. The tan SUV was nowhere to be seen.

Just as he breathed a sigh of relief and stretched his fingers, which had become cramped through his death-grip on the steering wheel, two cars appeared ahead of him, both at a dead stop in his lane as ahead of them, coming in the opposite direction, a gigantic tour bus inched its way around a corner too narrow to accommodate more than itself. He jammed on his brakes and came to a halt only inches from a blue Fiat 500 ahead of him, no doubt scaring the driver of the Fiat nearly to death. Within seconds the tan SUV pulled up behind him, nudging his bumper.

He was ready to leap from his car, gun in hand and accost the two men in the SUV but the tour bus was already beside his car, only inches away from his rearview mirror and leaving no room for him to open his door. At the same time the Fiat and a Volkswagen ahead of it began to move forward. He felt the SUV pushing on the bumper of his MINI Cooper. The turn was a sharp left-hander and the outside lane in which he was driving came within a few feet of the sheer cliff, high above the angry sea below. The SUV was pushing him closer and closer to the edge.

O'Reilly kept his foot on the brake, resisting the push of the SUV as much as the brakes of his MINI Cooper and his will power would allow, until the Fiat was ten yards ahead of him, the small car starting to round the curve. O'Reilly floored the gas pedal. His car leapt forward straight toward the edge of the road and the cliff below until, at the last minute, he managed to swing it around and, accelerating with all the power the tiny MINI Cooper could muster, he swung into the inside lane and brushed by the Fiat, missing the other car's door by inches, then doing the same to the Volkswagen ahead of it. Behind him the SUV screeched to a halt moments before its own momentum would have sent it over the cliff. O'Reilly breathed out the breath he had been 'holding since the moment his foot had pressed on the gas pedal and managed to chuckle to himself. With two cars between him and the SUV on the winding road, he would be able to stay safely ahead of it the rest of the way to Amalfi.

Although he was breathing easier, O'Reilly kept up his all-out assault on the cliffside road the rest of the way into Amalfi, passing several cars and even a motorcycle in the process. He felt exhilarated. His reflexes were more intact than he had imagined them to be, and he began to enjoy the thrill of the danger, eagerly anticipating every next curve in the narrow road high above the sea. When he spied Amalfi, nestled in a crack in the cliffs ahead and, in the setting sun, looking as if it were tumbling into the sea, he was more disappointed than relieved. He could have driven another ten miles just for the enjoyment.

Chapter 35

Whomever the men were in the tan SUV, he doubted that they had wanted to kill him. That meant it was probably not hit men from the *Camorra*, the interrelated clans of mafia-type gangs who controlled the *Campania* peninsula of Italy, which included Naples and Amalfi. The *Camorra* never flinched when it came to murder. The drivers of the SUV could have killed him on the road if that was their aim, although he wasn't completely sure about that, since he had left them in his dust before they had gotten the chance. For sure they wanted to let him know that he was not wanted in Amalfi. He had gotten the message.

He parked his MINI Cooper just outside the entrance to the town square but out of view of the main road, then walked to the town pier, where the ferry arrived daily and a number of sleek yachts were tied up. From there he could see every car that arrived on the road from Sorrento. Within minutes of his arrival at the pier, the tan SUV appeared on the narrow highway. It slowed, then stopped in the public parking area across from the pier. Two men emerged. Neither of them glanced toward the sea, where O'Reilly sat on the pier, his feet dangling over the water, looking as if he were one of the town locals or a tourist enjoying the salt air. When they turned to go into the town square, O'Reilly stood up and followed.

APPOINTMENT IN MYKONOS

The *Piazza del Duomo*, the central square of Amalfi was dominated by the ninth century Cathedral of St. Andrew or as it was also known, the *Duomo di Amalfi*. Its sixty-two steps, more than fifty feet wide, led steeply up to the Cathedral, which sat high above the square, purportedly over the crypt housing the remains of St. Andrew, brought from Constantinople after the fourth crusade. Lining the edges of the other three sides of the square were numerous restaurants and shops. No less than four streets converged on the square. O'Reilly watched as the two men from the SUV headed up the *Via Lorenzo d'Amalfi*, the main street leading back toward the mountains, which rose, like looming giants, behind the town.

Within a few hundred yards, the men turned off the *Via Lorenzo* into a narrow opening between two buildings; the opening distinguished only by a small sign with the words *Hotel Amalfi*. O'Reilly waited for a few moments, then peered around the corner into the opening. Steep stone stairs led upward to what looked like a narrow street on the level above. In the dying evening light, lamps had come on, lighting the stairway. A faint halo of ocean mist hung like an aura around each of the lamps as O'Reilly began his ascent. When he reached the top of the stairs he found himself at what amounted to a landing, which was the intersection of the staircase with a narrow street, too narrow for cars. Beyond, the stairway continued upward toward a street above. Immediately in front of him was a tiny restaurant with three tables set outside, invitingly lit by candles and with a fat, smiling waiter gazing at him, then gesturing for him to take a seat. He ignored the waiter and looked around. The door to the *Hotel Amalfi* was a few yards away. There was no sign of the men from the SUV.

He entered the lobby of the hotel, which was about the size of his cabin on the *Adriatic Voyager* and contained a registration desk, a potted plant and two chairs. A petite woman of about twenty-five, dressed in a crisp white blouse and a dark skirt and with a pleasantly oval face, piercing blue eyes and dark brown hair tied back severely in a ponytail, gazed at him expectantly.

"*Posso aiutarla?*" the woman asked in Italian.

"Do you speak English?" O'Reilly asked.

"*Si.* Of course," the woman answered.

"I'm looking for a friend. She's a young woman, Sylvia Marconi." He reached into the breast pocket of his coat and pulled out Julietta's picture. "This is her picture. She said she would be here at this hotel."

The woman glanced at the picture, then looked back at him, a troubled look clouding her striking blue eyes. "You said her name was Marconi?"

He realized that, since she had stayed at the hotel in the past, probably with her mother, Julietta would not have used her fictitious name. "It's a name she sometimes uses so no one recognizes her. She probably registered as Julietta Martini, her real name. She has been a guest here in the past… with her mother."

The woman smiled as if in relief. "Ah yes, Miss Martini. She came here several days ago. But you have missed her. She left the day before yesterday."

His spirits deflated. He had missed her.

"She didn't say where she was going did she?" he asked, although he already knew the answer to his question.

The young woman shook her head. "She said nothing." She paused as if debating whether to say more. "There were other men here asking about her," she said, ending her words with a sigh, as if her confession had taken a load off of her mind.

"When did the men come here?"

"Two days ago, soon after she left."

"What did you tell them?"

"Only that they had missed her. She had already checked out."

So the men in the SUV had not followed him to Amalfi; they already had been here. They were searching for Julietta too, but why had they stuck around for two days to wait for him? And who were they working for?

His hunch about her coming to Amalfi had been right on target, but he should have come here first instead of stopping in Florence to interview her roommates. Then he brightened. The two roommates had given him valuable information. If she was no longer in Amalfi, then her next destination was no doubt Mykonos. He at least had picked up her trail; he was now confident of that. Sergio Magetti had been wrong about her being abducted. Magetti was on a wild goose chase looking for her in Budapest.

But someone else was also looking for Julietta… someone who knew about the hotel in Amalfi.

He thanked the young woman and left the hotel. When he stepped outside, the two men from the SUV were waiting at the entrance to the stairway.

"I thought I'd never find you guys," O'Reilly said, a cheerful smile on his face. He walked purposely toward the two men, his hand extended as if to shake hands. "Where did you disappear to?"

They were both burly men, about his height but considerably heavier. They each wore light sport coats, dark slacks and heavy lace-up shoes. The one on his left was bald, but the one to his right had a full head of coal black hair. Both of them stared at him with puzzled expressions on their fleshy faces. He kept walking toward them, still smiling with his hand outstretched until he was within a yard of the one on his left and then he took one quick step and hit the man with a stiff left uppercut that seemed to come out of nowhere. The man teetered backwards toward the stairway, and O'Reilly followed up with a crossover right hand that knocked him backwards into the stairwell. The man staggered to keep his balance, but he lost his footing and tumbled backwards down the stone stairway, crying out in pain as he slid down the hard steps.

"Now its your turn," O'Reilly said, still smiling as he turned to the other man, who, instead of taking advantage of his adversary's preoccupation with demolishing his partner, had backed away. His face showed his alarm, but he was also reaching into his coat. Before O'Reilly could get to him, he had removed a large, black pistol.

O'Reilly swung his foot, catching the man's gun hand with his shoe and sending the pistol skittering across the cobblestones of the narrow street. The man's face showed his surprise. O'Reilly had won the light heavyweight division of the LAPD *Centurions'* mixed martial arts competition when he'd been on the force, and he'd kept up his skills. He landed in a crouch at right angles to his opponent then, using the coiled energy of his legs as a spring, he followed the first kick with a second, twisting his body and slamming the full force of his foot against the man's chest, staggering him backward. The thug clutched his chest in pain and O'Reilly' right hand caught him on the side of the head, driving him to the ground. By the time the man looked up, O'Reilly had his own gun pointing at the man's head.

"Who sent you?" he shouted at the stunned man on the ground. "Who are you working for?"

The man looked up at him but said nothing.

O'Reilly was unsure if the man understood English. He jammed his left foot on the man's neck and pinned him to the ground. Then he reached inside the man's coat and removed his wallet. Flipping it open, his foot still on the man's neck and his right hand still pointing his gun at his head, he looked for identification. What he saw left him stunned.

The man's identification showed him to be an employee of Martini Industries' Security Division. He worked for Alessandro Martini. What's more, that meant he worked for Sergio Magetti, who was the head of the Security Division.

What was going on?

As he asked himself these questions, he became aware of the crowd that had formed at the entrance to the restaurant, directly across from him. He looked up the street and saw that the young woman from the hotel also had come into the street. They were all staring at him. He heard someone murmuring about the *"polizia."* He realized that he was in the middle of a heavily trafficked tourist destination that was probably overloaded with police. He had a lot of questions, but no time to ask them. He took his foot off of the man's neck, then gave him a final kick in the head for good measure and turned and scurried down the stairway, leaping over the crumpled body of the other thug who had come to rest a few feet from the bottom of the staircase.

A crowd of people, mostly tourists, were standing at the bottom of the stairway looking up to see what was going on, and he pushed his way through them, muttering "police business," then moved as quickly as he could toward the *Piazza del*

Duomo, where he knew that he could lose himself in the thick crowd that still peopled the square.

He hurried through the crowded square, the large number of tourists oblivious to the disturbance that he had caused a little way up the *Via Lorenzo*. When he reached his car he backed out and headed back onto the *Amalfi Drive*, this time toward Salerno. He didn't think the security men he had beaten would say anything to the police, but he wanted to take a different route back to Naples, rather than repeat his experience of eluding the tan SUV on the winding *Amalfi Drive*. He was sure the two men had not given up their pursuit.

As he headed out on the still winding cliffside road, which would get him to Salerno in about a half hour, his thoughts turned to the question of why Sergio Magetti was trying to prevent him from finding Julietta Martini. Whoever it was that was employing the two men had known that Julietta was in Amalfi. Magetti had still been in Venice after O'Reilly had talked to Sophia Martini. She would have told him what she had told O'Reilly if Magetti had asked her. And he probably did.

But why was Magetti trying to stop him? Or was it Magetti? The security men ultimately worked for Alessandro Martini. Martini himself may have directed them to come to Amalfi. But Martini had never found out about his wife's and daughter's stay in the cliffside village. Or had he? And why would Alessandro Martini hire him to find his daughter and then send two thugs to stop him?

None of it made sense to O'Reilly. He only knew one thing: Julietta Martini was no longer in Amalfi and had probably gone on to Mykonos. Even Sophia Martini had not known that the island destination was a favorite of her daughter's. O'Reilly had gotten the information from Christina and Maria, Julietta's two Florence roommates. There was no reason the two security men, whomever they were working for, would go to Mykonos themselves. Not unless they were able to follow O'Reilly.

And he was determined not to let that happen.

APPOINTMENT IN MYKONOS

Chapter 36

Julietta Martini had been halfway across the
Piazza del Duomo when she'd seen the two men.
She'd recognized them from Sergio's security force.
What were they doing in Amalfi? She had paused
and watched them as they entered the *Via Lorenzo
d'Amalfi*. They were heading for the *Hotel Amalfi*,
the hotel from which she had just checked out. She
had stood there in the square, in front of the *Duomo
di Amalfi* feeling confused. The security men were
not supposed to know about Amalfi. Did this mean
that her father would soon know where she was?

Sergio's men might have discovered her
whereabouts in Amalfi, but no one would know
about Mykonos. No one but the young man she
was going to meet there and his aunt, the kindly old
woman who had hosted them on the island twice
before, when they had eluded her father's
surveillance and gotten away together for a
weekend from school.

She felt guilty about her mother. She had
always shared everything with her mother and her
mother had always protected her. It was her mother
who had put an end to Julietta's father's
inappropriate behavior toward his daughter when
she was younger… behavior that had frightened
and horrified her, but from which she could not
flee until her mother had managed to get Sergio to
watch her at every moment, keeping her father at a
distance because of the bodyguard's constant

surveillance. If it wasn't for her mother's courage, Julietta would have never known about the haven in Amalfi where the two of them had spent a week free of the domination of her father. But she hadn't told her mother about Mykonos. Besides the fact that her mother would disapprove of her affair with the young man, Julietta knew that her mother was at the mercy of her father. It pained Julietta to admit it, but her mother was unable to stand up to her father and was a prisoner within her own house. If Julietta's father thought that her mother knew where she was, he would force that information from her.

So she had not been able to tell her mother. Not even talk to her to tell her that she was safe. If the ruse with Dmitri had worked, her mother might even think that she had been kidnapped. After she had arrived in Amalfi, Julietta had cried herself to sleep every night, thinking about the pain she was causing her mother. She would not deliberately hurt anyone. She had never been able to. Her traumatic experiences with her father had left her forever vulnerable... polite and reserved to a fault. But she had backbone. She could be stubborn... and secretive. Keeping the secret of her father's unwanted advances toward her had made her cunning. But she never rebelled openly. The only time she had stood up to her father was when she had insisted on leaving Venice to attend university in Florence. But even then she had agreed to having Sergio continue to watch over her.

Sergio might have been ordered to keep Julietta under surveillance but that had not stopped her from growing into a young woman in Florence…a young woman who wanted desperately to seek a real relationship with a man, someone with whom she could share and trust. And she had done that, despite her father's watchful eye.

Now she and that young man were getting away, getting away completely.

She had taken the complicated route from Amalfi by bus across the "ankle" of the Italian peninsula to *Bari* where she had caught a ferry across the Adriatic to *Patras* on the Greek western coast and then another bus to Athens and finally a ferry from Athens to Mykonos. The trip had taken her two days, but here she was, finally in her lover's aunt's house in *Mykonos Town,* waiting for her young man to appear. Today was the day he would come. Today was the day her life would change forever.

APPOINTMENT IN MYKONOS

Chapter 37

For sure the two men in the tan SUV, who would soon be up and back on O'Reilly's trail—albeit a little worse for wear—had followed him from the Naples airport. But they had also been in Amalfi two days earlier, so they had not followed him from Florence. Sophia Martini had probably told Sergio Magetti that O'Reilly was headed for Amalfi, and Magetti could have instructed his men to wait for his arrival at the airport and follow him. But he still couldn't understand why Magetti would want to stop him from finding Julietta, assuming it really was Magetti and not Alessandro Martini himself who had dispatched the two men. At any rate, he wasn't going to return to the Naples airport and become a sitting duck for the two security men.

Rome was only two or three hours northeast of Naples and there were even more flights leaving from the *Leonardo DaVinci Airport* outside of Rome for the island of Mykonos than there were from Naples. The two men in the SUV wouldn't expect him travel to Rome, especially since he had rented his car in Naples, so they would try to catch him either on his way to or after he reached the rental agency at the Naples airport. He would fool them.

The A-1 highway was crowded but straight, and driving it in his MINI-Cooper was a relief after being chased along the winding *Amalfi Drive*, although O'Reilly had to admit that he missed the unexpected thrill he'd felt weaving in and out of the perilous curves high above the sea. When he reached the outskirts of Rome he merged onto the *Grande Raccordo Anulare*, or "*Il Raccordo*" as it was called locally, the ring road that encircled the city and led to the A-91 turnoff to the airport and the coastal city of Civitavecchia, where the *Adriatic Voyager* docked when it was in port. It was late evening and the ring road was teeming with traffic and off to the right, in the distance, he could see the lights on the hills of Rome, home of the ancient ruins of the *Colosseum*, the *Pantheon*, the *Forum* and the Baroque *Trevi Fountain*, not to mention, the *Vatican*. Even O'Reilly's jaded mind was able to generate a thrill at knowing that he was so close to so much history, but he also knew that he had no time to enjoy it. He had to reach Mykonos before Julietta escaped him again—or whoever was after him reached her first, although he had no idea what they would do if they did, or even if they already knew where she was and would be waiting for him in Mykonos. The last thought put him on his guard. He needed to be armed when he reached Mykonos. He would put his gun in his luggage, as he had done when he'd traveled from Florence to Naples and hope that that no one inspected his luggage.

The rental car agency complained about his returning his car to a different location from where he had rented it, but accepted it, nevertheless, although he had to pay a surcharge. He was prepared to put the charges on the Cruise Line credit card and then it occurred to him that he now knew how either Magetti or Alessandro Martini had known his whereabouts. They had traced his use of the Seven Seas Cruise Line credit card. He paid in cash. When he got to the airport he found that the first flight to Mykonos didn't leave until six in the morning. It was now after midnight. He debated getting a hotel, then decided that a sandwich and a drink in the airport bar, which was still open, would hold him until morning and he would find the most comfortable chair in the airport and just wait until the flight boarded at 5:30 a.m. The airport was uncrowded at that time of night and he found a set of seats that would allow him to lie down. But before he permitted himself the luxury of falling asleep he put in a call to Alessandro Martini.

"You're daughter's not in Budapest," he told Martini. "I tracked her to Amalfi, although she was gone when I got here."

"Where is she now?" Martini asked. He didn't appear surprised to hear that his daughter was in Southern Italy rather than Hungary.

"I have no idea." He had decided not to mention his theory that Julietta was in Mykonos. He still didn't know if Martini was or wasn't behind the effort to stop him from finding the man's daughter. "But two men with Martini Industries Security ID cards were waiting for me in Amalfi. They were looking for your daughter and they tried to run me off the road and beat me up."

"My security men?" Martini sounded confused. "I don't understand."

"Neither do I. They were working either for Sergio Magetti or for you."

"Working for me? Magetti's my Chief of Security. Everyone reports to him. But why would he try to stop you from finding Julietta?"

"I thought you might have an idea."

"Me? I'm flabbergasted. But I'm beginning to have a theory."

"Tell me."

"I haven't been able to reach Sergio for a couple of days. He's disappeared. I think the Budapest search was to lead me—and you—off the track. I think Sergio may have kidnapped Julietta himself."

Sergio was missing? And he had sent his men to interfere with O'Reilly's search for Julietta? "Why would he do that?" he asked.

Martini heaved a loud sigh on the other end of the telephone. "Money. Either he is going to ask for ransom, or he's working for one of my enemies who will use Julietta to blackmail me into some kind of business deal."

Martini's theory made sense. It explained Magetti's stubborn insistence on limiting his investigation to Budapest when it was obvious that Julietta wasn't there. It also explained why he would send someone to discourage O'Reilly's search for the young woman. But according to the hotel clerk, the two men had been looking for Julietta themselves the day before. If they were working for Magetti and Magetti had Julietta, why would they be looking for her? "You could be right, but some

226

things still don't make sense. And wherever your daughter is, we still have to find her.

"Where will you look next?" Martini asked.

"I don't know yet," O'Reilly lied. "I'm back in Naples and I'm going to look around here, since it's the closest big city to Amalfi and it's where Julietta disappeared from. I'll let you know if I find anything." He wasn't completely sure why he was giving Martini a false story, but he still had reservations about his employer's honesty with him. That Magetti might be behind the kidnapping was plausible on the surface, but parts of it still didn't make sense. The truth was, O'Reilly trusted no one at this point.

Despite his deep sense of disquiet over who was trying to stop him from finding Julietta Martini and whom he could trust, O'Reilly fell asleep almost the minute he put his head down on the airport lobby chair, and when he awoke in the morning he just had time to wash his face and brush his teeth before boarding his flight to Mykonos. There had been no sign of the two men from the SUV.

APPOINTMENT IN MYKONOS

Chapter 38

The small jet airliner held only about one-hundred passengers, and O'Reilly understood why when they landed at the small airstrip high on the top of the hills above the city of Mykonos. Around him were the waters of the blue Aegean and below, the white, flat-roofed houses and buildings of the town. He took a rickety taxi, driven by an overweight, red-faced man of indeterminate age, who talked expansively of the delights available in his island paradise. O'Reilly had imagined a sleepy Greek fishing village and he was astounded to hear from the driver about the numerous night spots where he might, or so it sounded, indulge almost any fantasy he might have.

"I just need a hotel—one that is central to the town," he interrupted the driver by asking in the middle of his soliloquy about the virtues of the different methods of drinking the signature drink of the Greek Islands, *Ouzo*: from straight with ice, to with water and ice, to straight and so cold it was nearly frozen.

"Oh, then if you want to stay in town, there are many clubs to go to in the main village or in *Little Venice*."

"Little Venice?"

"It is the best place to watch the sunset on the island. There are many restaurants and bars on the water. You must visit it at night."

228

O'Reilly didn't think that Julietta would be frequenting any of the bars or clubs, not if she was in hiding and staying with a friend. According to Christina and Maria, the friend was an old woman who lived on the island. Unless Julietta ventured out that would make it difficult for O'Reilly to find her. "Where do most of the permanent residents of the island live?" he asked the cab driver.

"Right here in the main town... except for a few rich newcomers who have built new houses at some of the beaches around the island: *Aglos Stefanos, Platys Gialos, Ornos.*"

He doubted that the old woman the girls in Florence had told him about was one of the new rich residents, which meant that she probably lived in town, but not knowing her name was going to make it hard to locate her. "How many permanent residents live here?" he asked. The island was awfully small and so was the town.

"About fifteen-thousand. Most of them are old families who have been here for generations... like mine."

"A friend of mine is staying with someone who lives here. She didn't tell me the woman's name but I know that she is old and I would guess that she lives by herself. Does that sound like anyone you know?"

"It sounds like at least a couple of dozen people I know. A lot of the young people leave the island, leaving their parents behind. There are a lot of older widows who remain here. Their kids come back now and then to visit, but most of the time they live alone." It sounded to O'Reilly as if Mykonos was like most of the idyllic vacation spots in the world, which seemed like the ideal place to live to tourists who only spent a week or two in them, but were boring and confining to the young people who grew up there.

O'Reilly pulled a fifty Euro bill from his wallet and handed it over the seat to the driver. "This is for checking around to see if any of those older widows has taken in a young Italian woman as a guest recently… in the last few days. That would help me find my friend."

"Why don't you just call your friend?" the driver asked, although he had taken the fifty.

"I don't know her cell phone number."

The driver shrugged. O'Reilly doubted if the man believed him, but he was willing to take the money, and if that meant that he would make inquiries, that was all that counted.

The taxi had come to a hotel, which was in the upper section of *Mykonos Town*, just below six large windmills, which the taxi driver explained to him were purely decorative but many years in the past had been used to mill wheat for the island's residents. *The Aegean* was a four stories high flat-roofed building, painted white just as were all the other buildings of the town. Above him, O'Reilly could see the balconies of rooms, which he could tell had magnificent views of *Mykonos Town*, and a long, narrow beach he was told was called *Megali Ammos* and was within walking distance. Beyond the beach the blue sea, dotted with numerous small

Greek islands, stretched to the skyline. O'Reilly had made no hotel reservation prior to grabbing the first morning flight out of Rome for the island, but this hotel was run by the cab driver's cousin and he had no difficulty securing a room.

The room itself was on the third floor, high enough to have a panoramic view of one side of the island. He could see not only *Mykonos Town* and the town beaches, but also the small port where a cruise ship as well as several commercial boats were docked. The bay directly in front of the town square was filled with both pleasure and fishing boats at anchor. The room itself was spacious. In addition to the king-size bed, there was a small couch and two sitting chairs and a coffee table and writing desk. French doors led out to the balcony. Much to O'Reilly's satisfaction, he had noticed a small bar in one corner of the lobby, although from what he had gathered from the cab driver's description of the town, he would find no shortage of bars.

Chapter 39

He unpacked his bags, then took a quick shower. He had been on the move from Florence to Amalfi to Rome to Mykonos and had even slept in the Rome airport so it had been a couple of days since O'Reilly had had a chance to shower and clean himself up. He changed into a clean set of clothes, although he didn't really have any beachwear, and emerged from his room wearing a pair of suntan slacks, a blue sports shirt with no tie, his loafers and a pair of sunglasses. He was ready to meet the town.

The town square at the bottom of the hill was less than a ten-minute walk and was crowded with open-air restaurants, all of them filled with vacationers having breakfast in the bright sunlight and crisp morning air and gazing out at the sparkling waters of the town harbor. He strolled past the tables, scanning all the restaurants for Julietta, although he didn't really expect to see her in such a public place. Then he picked a table that allowed him to watch the passersby as they enjoyed the walk through the square, which fronted directly on the harbor, which was filled with yachts and fishing boats. He had ordered coffee and breakfast but he had barely begun to eat when he saw a familiar face walking along the edge of the harbor. It was Sergio Magetti. The security man had not seen him yet.

APPOINTMENT IN MYKONOS

O'Reilly grabbed a newspaper off the table of the couple sitting next to him, who stared at him in horror while he held it up in front of his face and watched Magetti stride by. He looked like he knew exactly where he was going. What was the security chief doing here in Mykonos? Had he found out where Julietta Martini was headed and gotten here before O'Reilly? That was the only conclusion he could come up with. The question was whether Magetti had already found the young woman or was, like O'Reilly, still looking. Muttering a brief apology to the couple whose paper he had appropriated, O'Reilly put enough Euros on the table to cover his breakfast and slipped out from behind the table then followed Magetti at a safe distance.

Rounding the corner of the harbor, Magetti entered the section of the town known as *Little Venice*. Suddenly the street became nothing more than a tiny alley, barely wide enough for two people to pass. On either side of the street the buildings rose two or three stories, sometimes with shops on the ground floor, at other times with only small doorways leading, he assumed to residences. Side streets, no wider than the one he was on, led up the hill inland, with more shops and restaurants visible. He searched as far as he could see up the side streets but saw no sign of Magetti, so he assumed he must still be on the same narrow street that O'Reilly was following.

As he turned a corner, he came upon the sea. The waters of a small bay lapped against the stone walkway, which the street had become. Ahead he saw a crowded restaurant, its tables set only a few feet above the water. Beyond that he could see that more buildings fronted directly on the curving bay, their colorfully painted balconies suspended over the water. He caught a glimpse of Sergio Magetti turning up a side street that ran from the bay up the hill. He waited a moment, then followed.

Magetti was just entering a doorway up the hill ahead of him. The young security chief had stopped and was looking around before he entered. O'Reilly ducked inside the doorway of a tiny jewelry shop and waited. A middle-aged man with a magnifying glass attached to a leather band that encircled his head was seated at a workbench at the back of the shop working on a piece of jewelry. He turned his glass away from his eye and stared at O'Reilly. "Can I help you?"

O'Reilly smiled and shook his head. He made a quick show of looking over the contents of the shop, which consisted of a number of pieces of very expensive jewelry, then, glancing back to make sure that Magetti had entered the building, he smiled again and thanked the man and walked back out into the street.

Magetti's caution that he not be seen entering the house made it certain in O'Reilly's mind that Julietta Martini must also be in the house. Magetti must have found her already. That could only mean one thing: Alessandro Martini had been right: Sergio Magetti had kidnapped his daughter and was holding her captive. No wonder the security chief had sent his goons to stop O'Reilly in Amalfi. But who was Magetti working for? Was this his own operation? Was he going to demand ransom from his own employer? Or had he gone over to the side of one of Martini's enemies and kidnapped Julietta in some bizarre plan to blackmail Martini into a business decision? The only way O'Reilly could find the answer to his questions was to confront Magetti himself. But he couldn't risk Julietta in doing so.

Magetti would have had no way of knowing that O'Reilly knew about Julietta's fondness for Mykonos. Sophia Martini had never mentioned the island and O'Reilly had only found out about it when he talked to the roommates in Florence. So it was unlikely that Magetti would be expecting O'Reilly to show up on the island. But what was he supposed to do now? Even though he asked himself the question, O'Reilly knew the answer. He had to confirm the fact of Julietta's presence here on Mykonos. He knew that Sergio Magetti was here, but everything else was supposition. He couldn't report back to Alessandro Martini about his daughter's whereabouts unless he was one hundred percent sure that he had found her.

Chapter 40

The most direct way to find out if Julietta was in the house would be to walk up to the door and knock, but if Magetti was keeping Julietta prisoner inside the house, he would be keeping an eye on whoever approached the premises and that meant that he would see that it was O'Reilly. Magetti would have the advantage, being inside the house and O'Reilly on the outside and Magetti would know that he was there At this point, O'Reilly's being on the island without Magetti's knowledge was the only advantage the detective had.

He walked back to the café by the water. He could see that the shoreline curved back toward the hill on which sat the house that Magetti had entered. Did the house actually front on the bay? He entered the restaurant and asked for a table by the water. He had to wait for a few minutes for some customers who were just leaving, but then he was given a seat next to the railing that separated the tables of the restaurants from the clear water that washed against the stone porch on which they were perched. When he sat down he noticed that there was a narrow walkway just beneath the edge of the restaurant's porch and that the walkway continued around the corner. From his table he could see that around that corner was a small beach. He could not see the houses that fronted the beach, but from the location, it was almost certain that the house in which he presumed Julietta was being kept prisoner was one of them.

He ordered a gin and tonic and a plate of olives. When the waiter brought his order he asked about access to the beach.

"The beach is mostly used by the houses behind it, but you can take this small walk or one just like it on the other side of the beach, that runs all the way around the bay and reach the beach that way." He pointed to a small gate in the railing at the far end of the restaurant. "You can access the walkway here or back at the beginning of *Little Venice*. It is a public beach, so you are free to use it at any time."

He drank his gin and tonic, then ordered a second and finished his plate of olives. Leaving the restaurant, he walked along the narrow street toward the house on the hill, keeping out of sight and counting the separate buildings between the restaurant and the house where he assumed that Julietta was being kept. There were four houses between the restaurant and the house. Assuming that all of them faced the bay, he could easily identify which one he was interested in if he walked along the walkway and onto the beach.

He returned to the entrance to *Little Venice*. The walkway was not in plain sight and there was no sign indicating its location. He moved closer to the water and then caught sight of the small stone walk, completely unmarked but running just above the waterline, attached to the stone foundation of the first building. He looked down the narrow stone walkway, which ran like a lower lip beneath the buildings until it disappeared around the corner of the bay. It was just wide enough for a single person. He made a tentative first step onto the walkway, then began walking toward the beach.

He encountered no one, but passed two restaurants in addition to the one in which he had drunk his gin and tonics. Each time, his presence startled the diners who were sitting next to the bay and seemed unaware that there was a pathway running along the water's edge just below the level of their tables. The waiter who had served him smiled and nodded when he passed the last restaurant. Just around the corner, the walkway ended, although he saw that it resumed again on the other side of a small, sandy beach that was populated by more than a dozen bathers, with beach blankets and umbrellas. He didn't know if they were residents of the beachfront houses or interlopers, like himself.

There was no need for him to walk out onto the beach, since that would only put him in plain view of Magetti if the security man was looking out from the house. O'Reilly had no difficulty identifying which house was the fourth one after the restaurant. Virtually all of the houses had windows open to the sea—windows that would also afford a view of anyone on the beach—as well as doors leading from each house to the sand. He kept his head down and scanned the bathers at the beach, hoping, but not really expecting, to see Magetti or Julietta among them. He assumed that

Julietta was being kept prisoner, but she and Magetti also had a relationship from the past. The security officer might have insinuated himself into her life by helping her to run away from her father without betraying his motives as a kidnapper. If that was the case, then the house belonged to the old woman who was Julietta's friend and Julietta might be free to go onto the beach in plain sight of Magetti's eyes. It was difficult to tell from a distance if she was one of the people on the beach and nearly everyone in sight was wearing sunglasses. He could move closer for a better look, but if Julietta was not one of the sunbathers, then he would risk being seen by Magetti, who no doubt was keeping a close watch on the young woman. He decided to wait.

Back in his hotel room O'Reilly prepared himself for his evening adventure. He hadn't brought any equipment for entering second floor windows and the thought of buying a ladder then carrying it along the walkway in front of numerous buildings, including three restaurants, made no sense to him, even if he waited until after midnight. He had heard that nightlife on the island often lasted until nearly dawn, so there was no guarantee that the restaurants, or at least their bars, wouldn't be filled no matter what time of night he passed by them.

But he did have his lock picks: a small set of variously shaped picks that folded into a clasp that he always carried attached to his key ring. The back door to the house probably entered into a basement of some sort, since the main floor was no doubt on the level of the street in front of it and the back door led directly to the beach. He could enter the house and probably not be detected until he reached his destination, which would be Julietta's room, wherever that was. There were probably two other people in the house: Magetti seemed to be working alone, but there was also the old woman who owned the house, assuming that the security officer had not moved Julietta from where she had been staying on the island. He wondered if the old woman too, was a prisoner. Or perhaps an accomplice. At any rate, O'Reilly figured he had a one-third chance of entering the right room. He didn't want to frighten the old woman who owned the house, but if he walked in on Sergio Magetti, he would have no difficulty handling the security officer and getting him to lead him to Julietta. The main thing was that, in the middle of the night, and caught by surprise, Magetti would have no chance to spirit Julietta away.

APPOINTMENT IN MYKONOS

Chapter 41

O'Reilly ate a hearty dinner of sea bass and rice at a restaurant a few blocks from his hotel, then went back to the hotel and had a gin and tonic in the lobby bar before going to his room and lying down on his bed to wait until after midnight. At one in the morning, he awoke. He slipped on his shoes and walked to the balcony. Below him, the streets leading down to *Mykonos Town* were well lit. A light sea fog covered the tops of the buildings in *Little Venice*. The flat rooftops rising above the mist resembled a fairyland perched among the clouds.

When he emerged from his hotel he was surprised to find that the streets were crowded— almost as crowded as they had been that morning. Most of those walking around, some with drinks or bottles of beer in their hands, were young people, in their twenties or thirties, obviously partying. He passed several clubs from which loud dance music was blaring into the street. He reminded himself that this was not the place to vacation if someone was looking to get away from the noise and bustle of city life. The young people had brought that life with them, at least at night.

Little Venice was quieter. The fog was more dense than it had appeared from his hotel and he could just make out the outlines of the buildings where the walkway began. The sea had risen with the tide and he could hear the rhythmic slap of the waves against the foundations of the houses. With the higher tide there were places where the water washed across the narrow stone walkway making the surface more slippery than it had been earlier in the day and soaking his shoes. The night air was cool and he felt the caress of the ocean mist on his face. There was a smell of salt in the damp air. The shuttered shops were bright outlines in the gray fog as he edged along the narrow shelf below the buildings. When he passed the first restaurant, emerging from the fog like a ghostly creature from the sea, he nearly scared the diners to death. When he reached the beach, it was shrouded in fog.

He counted the houses, barely visible in the gray mist, starting at the restaurant, until he recognized the vague outline of the fourth house. With no lights in any of its windows, it loomed like the dark outline of a ghost in the gloomy fog. He walked along the edges of the houses, keeping out of sight of the house where Julietta was being kept, until he came to the doorway that led into the house from the beach. The door handle was slick with moisture and locked.

It took him less than a minute to gain entrance to the house. As soon as he was inside, he used the flashlight on his cell phone to assess where he was. He found himself in a basement, just as he had expected, filled with brooms, beach chairs and umbrellas, and a few pieces of what was apparently discarded indoor furniture. Ahead of him was a stone stairway leading up to the main floor. The door at its top was closed.

He climbed the stairway. The sand that had stuck to his wet shoes crunched against the stone stairs. The door at the top was unlocked and he turned the knob and pushed it open. He was greeted by more darkness, although not so complete as in the basement. Weak light from the street shown through the light curtains on the window in the next room. He closed the door behind him and looked around. He was in a kitchen. There was a strong smell of garlic in the air.

He put his cell phone back in his pocket and waited until his eyes adjusted to the semi-darkness. The next room was a dining room and beyond that, a living room, from which the light was shining from the street. He assumed that the bedrooms were upstairs. He moved through the dining room and into the living room. Next to the doorway from the dining room was a staircase leading to the next floor. He stopped and listened. He could hear the sound of snoring coming from the floor above.

The stairs were wooden, and O'Reilly crept slowly upward, easing himself from stair to stair to avoid the creak of their ancient wood. When he reached the top he stopped and listened. The snoring was coming from his left. He moved down the hallway toward his right and passed an open bathroom door, then came to the first bedroom. There was a fifty-fifty chance that this was Julietta's room.

When he listened through the door he heard nothing. How was he to know if this was the bedroom of the old woman who owned the house or was the room in which Julietta was staying? The only thing he knew for sure was that it wasn't Sergio Magetti's room. The loud snoring down the hall had been a dead giveaway to the security officer's location.

He took a deep breath and turned the handle on the door, then slowly pushed it open. He heard nothing but silence from inside the room. He waited, listening for the sound of breathing. Nothing. Across the room was a single bed. He moved toward it, holding his breath, searching the darkness with his eyes. A pale light entered the room from a curtained window that no doubt looked out on the sea. He finally reached the bed and looked down.

The bed was empty.

How many bedrooms did the house have? He moved stealthily back to the door and stepped into the hallway. There was only one more door before the hallway ended. Were there more bedrooms in the other direction? He moved back along the hallway until he reached the staircase. The hallway leading in the other direction was shorter. There was only one door.

The house had but three bedrooms. One of them was empty. Either the old woman or Julietta was not in the house. Now he had no choice. He moved in the direction of Magetti's room. The security officer was the key to Julietta's location, and O'Reilly was determined to do whatever was necessary to wring the information out of him.

The room was flooded by weak moonlight shining in through an open, curtainless window, which also let in the cool, damp air. The air smelled of saltwater. In one corner was a large bed, much larger than the one in the other bedroom. The snoring was coming from the bed. O'Reilly crept across the floor. He took his gun from where it was tucked into his belt and held it ready. He had no intention of shooting Magetti, but he had every intention of threatening him. When he reached the side of the bed, he looked down at the sleeping security officer. The man's mouth was wide open, with loud, nasal sounds coming with every breath. He poked him in the shoulder with his gun.

Magetti woke with a start. "*Madre di Dio!*" He grabbed at O'Reilly's gun hand and at the same time rolled out of bed.

O'Reilly jerked his hand away, still holding onto the gun. Magetti was lying on the floor, looking up at him as if debating his next move. O'Reilly pointed the gun at him. "Just stay there or I'll shoot," he said.

"No!" The female voice came from the bed and O'Reilly looked up, startled. A blonde-haired slim woman was sitting up in bed, holding the covers over her chest. Her face was contorted in terror, but he recognized her immediately.

The face was that of Julietta Martini.

Chapter 42

"You can't tell my father." Julietta Martini was huddled against Sergio Magetti, but this time they were both sitting up in bed, Julietta still holding the covers up to her neck to cover herself.

"Tell your father what? That Sergio is holding you captive, or that you're in with him on this kidnapping plan?"

"Kidnapping?" the young woman asked, looking confused. "I wasn't kidnapped. Sergio and I made that up. I'm hiding from my father. So is Sergio."

"Can you leave and let us get dressed?" Magetti growled irritably. His flashing eyes betrayed the depths of his anger.

"Right," O'Reilly answered. "I'll just step outside while you two get dressed. And Sergio will no doubt not only dress but grab his gun and might even shoot me. You sent a couple of men after me in Amalfi, didn't you, Sergio?"

Julietta looked at Magetti in shock. "You sent your men after him? That's why those two men were in Amalfi, checking my hotel?"

Magetti looked embarrassed. "They were only supposed to scare him off, not hurt him." He looked back at O'Reilly. "Anyway, you were the one who beat up my men. Guido had to go to the hospital to get stitches where you kicked him in the face. Marco almost broke his leg."

"They weren't very good at their job."

"Well this is embarrassing to Julietta. She needs to put some clothes on."

O'Reilly looked at the young woman. She was afraid to look him in the eyes. She pulled the bedcovers up even higher as if to protect herself.

"O.K." he said. "Sergio, you get out of bed and put on some pants and come downstairs with me. Julietta can get dressed then come down and join us." He looked over at her. "But if you're not down in five minutes, then I'm coming in after you… right after I hurt your boyfriend here."

Julietta looked relieved, but frightened.

"You don't have to threaten her," Magetti said angrily.

"I'm not threatening her I'm threatening you. I owe you a beating, Sergio, and it will take very little to convince me to give it to you."

"I won't try to run away," Julietta said. "What good would it do? You already now about Sergio and me and you'll just tell my father."

Magetti got out of bed and pulled on a pair of pants and an undershirt, then walked out of the bedroom. O'Reilly followed with his gun still drawn. They descended the staircase.

"What about the old woman who owns the house?" O'Reilly asked, when they had reached the living room and both of them were seated in a pair of wooden-back antique chairs.

"My aunt Leonora? She lives here alone."

"Your aunt? I thought you were Italian."

"I'm Greek on my mother's side. She's my mother's older sister. My mother is from Mykonos.

Her sister never married. She stayed here in the family house. My grandparents died several years ago and she has the house to herself."

"So the friend of Julietta's who owns this house is your aunt?"

Magetti nodded.

"So tell me about you and Julietta."

Magetti looked at him, the anger still evident in his eyes. Then he looked down, as if embarrassed. "We're in love. Her father would have me killed if he found out. She's not supposed to marry the help."

"Martini thinks you've kidnapped his daughter."

Magetti's jaw dropped. "He thinks I kidnapped her? Why would I do that?"

"For money or because you're working for someone else… one of his rivals."

"I wouldn't do that." His face showed his horror.

O'Reilly was revising his assessment of the situation. "That's what you two planned to do? Get married?"

"We had to get away first…somewhere where her father couldn't find us."

"So you cooked up the story that she had been kidnapped. That worked for awhile. You might even have been able to sell the idea that she had died or at least was never to be heard from again. But once you disappeared yourself, you blew it. Now Martini suspects you."

Magetti shrugged. "We've been playing it by ear. We had planned to run away. I was going to join her after she left the boat at Naples. But when I found out about Dmitri Dragic and his connection to sex trafficking, I decided to take advantage of the situation and act as if Julietta had been kidnapped."

"And you had to kill Dragic so he wouldn't be able to say he hadn't taken Juliettta—only Marina."

Magetti's eyes flashed again in anger. "Dragic was a cockroach. He kidnapped innocent girls and turned them into drug-addicted prostitutes. He tried to kill both you and me . He deserved to die."

"Maybe he did, but you killed him so he couldn't talk."

Magetti shrugged. "I shot him so he wouldn't shoot you."

There was a sound on the stair and they both turned. Julietta was coming down the staircase in a short dress. She had combed her hair. She was barefoot. O'Reilly saw that, even without makeup, she was a beautiful young woman. Her blonde hair, which was like her mother's, came to below her shoulders and hung in loose waves. She had fair skin and large, dark eyes. Her nose and chin were narrow but not long. Her mouth was wide, with full lips. She was slim but her legs, below the short dress, were shapely.

"You can't let my father know about us. He will kill Sergio. He will make me a prisoner as he has my mother." She came across the room and sat down on a small satin couch facing the two of them. She crossed one leg over the other and stared at O'Reilly.

O'Reilly didn't doubt the truth of her words. But he wondered if she really loved Magetti or had just used him to help her get away from her father.

"You don't mind if I remain a little skeptical do you? Sergio has lied to me about you from the get-go, and he sent a couple of thugs to beat me up when I was just doing my job. Your father thinks that Sergio has kidnapped you, which was my opinion also until I found the two of you in bed together. This has all been a little mind-boggling for a simple detective like myself."

She looked startled. "But we're telling the truth. Sergio and I planned to run away to this island for months. You can ask his aunt. She knew that we were coming. My father knows that Sergio didn't kidnap me. That's an absurd idea. My father wants me back and he probably has begun to suspect that Sergio and I are together. I'm sure that's why he told you that Sergio had kidnapped me."

"He would have found you out eventually."

Her eyes flashed in defiance. "Not until we were married. It would have been too late by then."

"Would it?" O'Reilly cast a sidelong glance at Magetti.

"He would probably have me killed.... even if we were married," Magetti said. He cast a guilty glance toward Julietta.

It was Julietta who now had the look of horror on her face.

"So that was your plan? A happy but short life together?" O'Reilly asked.

"I thought we might go to Asia or South America," Magetti answered. "Martini has few contacts in those parts of the world." His tone didn't suggest that he had any faith in such a plan.

"If we announce our wedding in the newspapers, my father won't dare to do anything. He hates publicity."

"Would that stop him?" he asked, looking at Magetti.

The security chief again shook his head. "He would make sure that my death looked like an accident. Our only hope is to go somewhere he will never find us."

"And what will you live on? Julietta is the daughter of a billionaire. Someday that will all be hers, but not if you and she run away. Her father will disinherit her."

"We don't need her money!" Magetti growled. "I can earn a living. I can support us."

"As what? A cop? A bodyguard? Don't you think your employer would do a background check? Then he'd contact her father."

"I can work," Julietta said quietly. "I'm working on my degree in literature and I know a lot about art."

O'Reilly softened his voice. "Those are not highly employable skills, I'm afraid. And again, a museum or reputable employer would need to contact your school for verification. Eventually your father would find out."

Magetti looked ready to burst. "We can get along," he said angrily. "I can drive a taxi, or work as a bouncer, or whatever. We'll find a third world country where it's cheap to live."

"Is that the kind of life you want?" O'Reilly asked.

Before either of them could answer, there was a sound on the staircase. Reflexively, O'Reilly's hand went to his gun.

"It's my aunt," Magetti whispered, holding out a hand to stop O'Reilly from drawing his gun.

The woman on the stairway stopped and looked at the three of them. She said something O'Reilly didn't understand in Greek.

Magetti answered back in Greek, then spoke in English. "This is a friend of ours, *Thia*," he said. "We are just talking. Sorry to disturb you. You can go back to bed."

The woman, who was dressed in a bathrobe looked at her nephew disapprovingly. She was white-haired with a wrinkled face and looked to be in her sixties. "You have a guest and you don't offer him any tea or coffee?"

"He's not staying long, Thia," Magetti said, his tone softened for the sake of the old woman.

"Coffee sounds great to me," O'Reilly said, looking appreciatively at the woman on the staircase.

"See, Sergio. Your guest wants coffee," the woman said and smiled at O'Reilly, then descended the rest of the way and padded into the kitchen.

"What are you going to do?" Magetti asked, looking defiantly at O'Reilly.

"I have to tell Julietta's father that I've found her."

"You can't!" the young woman said, her voice pitched high in fear.

"I'll find a way to stop you," Magetti growled.

"I doubt that," O'Reilly answered, looking straight at Magetti. "But anyway, I won't tell Martini anything until we find a way for you two to not get hurt. OK?"

Julietta looked at him eagerly. Magetti looked more skeptical. "How will you do that?"

"I've got to think about it."

"Coffee everyone?" Magetti's aunt announced, entering the room with a tray loaded with three cups of coffee.

Chapter 43

The flight from Mykonos to Venice's *Marco Polo Airport* took only two and a half hours, but it was enough time for O'Reilly to worry himself into serious questions about the feasibility of his plan. The lives of two people were depending on the plan's success, and even though he had finally convinced both Sergio and Julietta that their only chance was to trust in him, he wasn't at all sure that he would be able to justify their confidence.

Magetti's old contacts with the Naples *Polizia*, for whom he had worked before joining Alessandro Martini's staff, had come in handy. The Naples police department hadn't been the ones conducting the investigation on the death of Marcello Bertolini, the gambler from the cruise ship, but they knew everything about it. Despite a half a million Euro reward being offered by Bertolini's wealthy family for any information leading to the arrest of his killers, no one had come forward. The *Carabinieri* were still not aware of Bertolini's presence on the *Adriatic Voyager*, much less that he had won a large sum of money by cheating on roulette—something for which Tony Braga, the man in charge of the ship's private gaming room, a man who reported directly to Alessandro Martini, had vowed to make Bertolini pay. According to Sergio's contacts within the *Polizia*, the *Carabinieri's* investigation of Bertolini's murder had reached a dead end. They were eager for a lead, any lead.

The plane touched down and O'Reilly took his small carry-on bag and boarded the *vaporetto* for Venice's *Terminal Passeggeri*, the cruise ship terminal at the foot of the *Ponte della Liberta*, the bridge leading from the mainland to Venice's interconnected islands. Seven Seas Cruise Lines' offices and warehouses were located at the cruise terminal and for this visit, Alessandro Martini had asked O'Reilly to meet him at his business location, rather than at his residence on the Grand Canal.

Seven Seas Cruise Lines had its own dock for *vaporetti*, water taxis and for Alessandro Martini's private powerboat, in which the owner commuted from his home each morning. Only a dock away were the terminals for the major cruise lines that visited the city. There were four cruise ships tied up at the terminals, although none of them was the *Adriatic Voyager*, which would arrive in another week after visiting Istanbul, Ephesus and Athens.

O'Reilly was greeted on the dock by a heavyset Italian in a dark suit and sunglasses, who introduced himself only as Sebastiano before he pointed toward the glass door of the three story building that was the cruise line's offices and directed O'Reilly inside. The glass-enclosed foyer of the building had a highly polished marble floor with a ten-foot long replica of the *Adriatic Voyager*, the company's signature ship, in the middle of the room and a semicircular white marble reception desk off to one side. At the back of the foyer was a shiny metallic elevator. The young female receptionist at the desk merely nodded as Sebastiano pointed for O'Reilly to proceed directly to the elevator door. When he entered the elevator, Sebastiano stepped in behind him and pushed the button for the third floor.

O'Reilly stepped out of the elevator into another reception area, this time with no desk but with a pair of black leather couches on either side of a low metal coffee table and behind them, two corridors leading to, he assumed, offices. Sebastiano motioned for him to take the corridor on his right and he proceeded to the end of the corridor. When he arrived in front of a door at the end of the hallway, Sebastiano gave a short knock and then turned the handle. Alessandro Martini was seated at a wide, cherrywood desk, a desk which, just as the desk in his home, was devoid of clutter or apparent work, with the exception of an in and out box, both of which were half-full with papers. Martini was dressed in an elegant dark wool suit with a light blue shirt and a plain cream-colored tie. He came around his desk with his hand outstretched toward O'Reilly.

"Thank you for coming to my office," Martini said, shaking O'Reilly's hand and motioning for him to take a seat opposite him in one of the two dark red leather chairs in front of his desk. "It is less comfortable here than at my home, but alas, I could not leave work this morning. The *Adriatic Voyager* is in Istanbul where they are having some civil unrest, which has disrupted our excursion schedule and we have ships leaving both Barcelona and Rome today. This afternoon I must meet with our advertising team to finalize plans for our next year's campaign. We are adding another ship to our fleet and it requires constant effort to keep all of the ships fully booked throughout the season."

O'Reilly smiled but said nothing. He detected a brittle edge beneath Martini's outward friendliness. Did he already know about his daughter and Magetti?

"You're here about Julietta," Martini said, looking him steadily in the eyes. "I guess you have found her but you do not have her with you, so I assume there is still a problem with her returning."

"How did you know that I found her?" O'Reilly asked, returning Martini's stare.

"Sergio's men may report to him but they work for me. I learned that Sergio and my daughter were together some time ago."

"But you didn't do anything?"

Martini's mouth curled in a smile, although his eyes remained hard. "I didn't know where they were. After Amalfi, Sergio stopped communicating with his men."

"So you still don't know where your daughter is?"

He raised one eyebrow. "I didn't know where she was until this morning. The flight on which you arrived was from Mykonos. I assume that Julietta is there... and Sergio is with her."

"Do you still think he kidnapped her?"

"I never did."

"What are you planning to do?"

"I have sent some men to bring Julietta back home."

"And Sergio?"

Martini's mouth again curled into a cruel smile. "Sergio will not return home."

"Much like Marcello Bertolini."

Martini's face drained of its color. "I don't have any idea who you are talking about?"

"Bertolini was a guest on the *Adriatic Voyager*. He cheated your private gaming room out of thirty-five thousand dollars at the roulette wheel. After he disembarked from the ship, he was murdered in Naples. The *Carabinieri* haven't found any clues to his death but of course they are unaware of his presence on the *Voyager* and his good fortune in cheating your ship of its money."

Martini looked at him with narrowed eyes. "You have no proof of any of that."

"Don't I? I am an eyewitness to his presence on your ship and I watched him cheat at the roulette wheel. Afterward I heard your employee, Tony Braga say that he would make Bertolini pay for such behavior. And I am willing to testify to that. The *Carabinieri*, of course, can simply investigate the records on the *Voyager* and find that Bertolini was not only a passenger, but that he was paid a large sum as winnings from the shipboard casino only a few days before he was murdered. I am sure that with such leads, they will find even more evidence tying you to the murder."

Martini began to laugh. "I admire your audacity Mr. O'Reilly. You sit in the middle of my office and threaten me by saying that you can provide the *Carabanieri* with information implicating me in a murder. Do you think I will let you leave here after such a threat?"

O'Reilly smiled back at him. "I'm sure you will."

Martini looked curious. "And why would I do that?"

"Because I've written down everything that I know, and Sergio Magetti has been instructed to give that information to the *Carabanieri* if I do not return to Mykonos safely."

"But poor Sergio will not be able to deliver your information I am afraid. My men are landing in Mykonos as we speak."

"I hope they have a good time there. The night life is great. But neither Sergio nor your daughter is on the island."

For the first time, anger showed on Martini's face. "Where have they gone?"

"Nowhere you will be able to find them," O'Reilly was still smiling.

Martini jumped up from his chair and went to the door. He opened it and called Sebastiano's name.

The burly Italian entered the room and looked inquiringly at his employer

"Sebastiano, take Mr. O'Reilly to the East Terminal warehouse. Take some men with you. He has some information we need to get from him."

Sebastiano headed toward O'Reilly, who stood up to face him. "This isn't a smart move Sebastiano," O'Reilly said, his smile not having left his face.

Sebastiano muttered something in Italian and reached a large hand out to grab O'Reilly by the shoulder. O'Reilly's left hand caught him under the chin and sent him reeling backward. Before he could straighten up O'Reilly's right fist, delivered with enough force to have downed a steer, smashed against the side of his head. He went down in a heap.

"I'm surprised at you Martini," O'Reilly said. He wasn't even breathing heavily. "Such a plush office is no place to use strong arm tactics. You're lucky nothing got broken… other than Sebastiano's jaw."

Martini had backed away and was on the other side of his desk. There was fear as well as anger in his eyes. "I have more men. You cannot win."

"Oh yes I can. As I said, if I do not return safely, Sergio will give my information to the *Carabinieri*. And trust me… your men will not get Sergio's location from me. They'd be lucky to even get me to that warehouse you mentioned."

Martini wrestled with his anger. Then his shoulders slumped and he gazed at O'Reilly with a beaten look on his face. "What do you want from me?"

"I want you to let your daughter and Sergio Magetti be married. And I want you to allow that marriage to continue without you doing anything to harm Magetti."

Martini's face was red with anger. "Married? She and Sergio? That's absurd. Sergio is my employee. He is a simple bodyguard. She can't marry someone like that."

"They are in love."

Martini had gotten over his shock but not his anger. "What has that got to do with anything? I didn't make all of this money to have my daughter marry someone who works for me." He gave O'Reilly a hard look. "Magetti has sealed his fate. I cannot brook this kind of audacity from one of my employees."

"And your daughter's feelings?" O'Reilly asked him.

"Her feelings count for nothing. She is a mere child. She doesn't know what she feels."

O'Reilly surveyed him with a cool gaze. "I think she knows exactly how she feels. She is in love with Sergio and he is in love with her. It has been difficult for her to trust a man enough to love him because she had some difficult childhood experiences, which she told me about. But Sergio has gained her trust and her love."

Martini's eyes narrowed. "What did she tell you?"

"Enough to let me know that your are not a fit father."

Martini squirmed in his chair. He looked as if he was going to have a seizure or a stroke. Then his shoulders slumped further. "That was many years ago," he said, his voice so weak that O'Reilly could barely hear him. "I was younger, I had pressures, I drank too much back then. It was not me."

"It will always be you in your daughter's mind. She fears you and she hates you. But she is your daughter also. You could extend an olive branch."

"By letting her marry Sergio Magetti?"

"He is a good man. He loves your daughter. He has spent his career protecting her."

"I don't like to lose."

"Think of it as winning. You're not losing a daughter—one you already lost, by the way—you are gaining a son-in-law."

Martini looked at him suspiciously. "And what do you want for yourself?"

O'Reilly shrugged. "My fee for finding your daughter. I think that's fair. I did what I was hired to do."

Martini leaned back in his chair. "You are a strange man, Mr. O'Reilly. Anyone else would have tried to blackmail me with the information you possess."

"I *am* blackmailing you. I am asking you to let your daughter marry Sergio Magetti."

"A small price to pay for keeping your silence. But I expected you to ask for money."

"I did. I want to be paid my fee."

"And so you shall."

O'Reilly looked at him evenly. "Give me your word that Sergio and Julietta will be unharmed and allowed to marry."

Martini nodded. "You have my word."

"Then I'll be leaving. Your daughter and Sergio will return within a day." He looked up at Martini and narrowed his eyes. "And my testimony will be put somewhere safe where it can be used in case something happens to them or to me."

Martini waved his hand. "You have won. You needn't make threats. I may play rough but I play fair. Once I have given my word, a deed is finished."

O'Reilly turned and walked out the door.

Chapter 44

The musical fanfare from the six French Horns sent the pigeons in the *Piazza San Marco* soaring into the blue Italian sky above the basilica. A line of guests formed a sinuous trail of humanity which stretched from the entrance of the 17th century cathedral to the middle of the plaza. Brian O'Reilly and Anka Sokolov stood near the head of the line, shuffling through the tall arched doorway into the inner church, and gazed at each other.

"You never told me the whole story of how you found Julietta and how she ended up with Sergio Magetti," Anka said, looking up at him. "And how did you merit a VIP invitation to the wedding?" She had met O'Reilly at the *San Zaccaria* dock after taking the *vaporetto* from the newly arrived *Adriatic Voyager.*

"Hey, I found the boss' daughter. That merit's something."

"I suppose so. So tell me again how you found her?"

"She ran away so she could marry Sergio. I found them both and talked her father into letting them get married." He looked at her with a smug expression. "Simple story."

"So you're a matchmaker as well as a detective?"

"I'm very versatile."

The line moved into the church and he and Anka were escorted to a pew near the front, behind

264

Julietta's family. Sophia Martini turned around and smiled at O'Reilly then mouthed the words, *mille gracias.* Across the aisle a burly man and a group of women and children dressed in brand new tight outfits in which they were obviously uncomfortable, looked uneasily toward the altar. Sergio Magetti's father, a former Naples policeman, had brought not only his wife, but all of his son's siblings and cousins to the wedding.

Ted Firestone squeezed into the pew next to O'Reilly. He too, had just arrived, but had had to greet his employer and his wife before joining his friends. "Congratulations. You found Julietta, you humanized Sergio, and I still have a job, but Martini doesn't seem very happy with you, bro."

"He's a sore loser."

"What did he lose?"

"He didn't get to torture me."

Firestone stared at him. "It came that close?"

"I was winging it at the end, but I had him in a corner. My bluff was stronger than his."

"But he paid you?"

"I did the job didn't I?"

"So how come you're invited to the wedding? It sounds as if Martini isn't too fond of you."

"I'm a guest of the bride and groom. Screw Martini."

Firestone chuckled. "You never change."

"That's good," Anka piped up. She had been listening attentively to their banter.

Firestone smiled. "I agree, Miss Sokolov, I agree."

The ceremony was long and, to O'Reilly, boring. The only bright spot was when Alessandro Martini walked his daughter down the aisle. Julietta, for her part, looked gorgeous in a white wedding gown with a train as long as a Mercedes limousine, held up at its ends by two of Sergio's young nieces. Martini looked pleased in spite of himself. That is until he spied O'Reilly in the audience. If looks could kill, O'Reilly would not have survived the wedding.

"I guess you won't be rehired," Firestone whispered to him.

O'Reilly shrugged. "He'll get over it."

After a short trip across the *Giudecca Canale* in a private water bus, the wedding party, including O'Reilly and his friends, disembarked at a dock on one end of *Giudecca Island* in front of the *Hilton Molino Stucky,* the massive, late 19th century flour mill turned into a luxury hotel, whose rooftop poolside restaurant was the site for Julietta Martini's, now Mrs. Julietta Magetti, wedding reception. The reception line was long and the newly married couple was showing their fatigue after the 100th guest offered his congratulations. But when O'Reilly and Anka finally reached the spot in front of them, the young couple brightened. Julietta threw her arms around O'Reilly, then after disengaging herself, gave Anka a warm hug. "Keep him close," Julietta said to Anka in a stage whisper. "My roommate from Florence is here and she's got her eye on your man." Anka didn't look worried.

Magetti gave O'Reilly's hand a solemn shake. "I was wrong about you," he said.

"That's OK," O'Reilly answered. "We're not all the assholes we seem to be." He glanced down the line toward Julietta's father. "Not all of us."

He moved down the line toward Alessandro Martini. When he reached him, the tycoon gave him a stony stare.

"Congratulations," O'Reilly said. "This may be the best thing that's happened to your family, so cheer up." He didn't offer his hand.

Sophia Martini, standing next to her husband and looking stunning in a pale yellow dress, whose hue matched the blonde of her hair perfectly, put both of her arms around O'Reilly and gave him a warm hug. "Thank you for bringing our daughter back to us," she said. "Someday my husband will realize how valuable what you did for us was." She looked at her husband next to her and stared him in the eyes, exuding a new-found confidence that O'Reilly had not seen before.

O'Reilly introduced Anka to Julietta's mother and told her how helpful Anka had been in helping to locate her daughter. Then he and Anka moved off toward the tables scattered around the edge of the rooftop patio, which afforded a 360° view of the surrounding area, including the towers and rooftops of central Venice across the canal and the long, low *Lido Island* behind them. Circulating waiters were delivering drinks to the seated and standing guests. Ted Firestone, who was holding a table for the two of them, sat with two drinks in front of him. When O'Reilly and Anka reached his table he handed a gin and tonic to O'Reilly then asked Anka what she would like to drink.

"I feel a little awkward being served by my captain," Anka said with a nervous smile.

"Don't be. I just served the Irish troublemaker you're with, and he's a wedding crasher as far as the bride's father is concerned. If I go to the bar I can have them make you a Bellini. I've heard that this place's Bellinis are as good as those at Harry's Bar."

"How can I refuse?" Anka said, overcoming her embarrassment. She turned to O'Reilly. "The captain doesn't seem afraid to be seen with you, even though Mr. Martini obviously hates your guts." Anka said.

"Are you worried that being with me could affect your career?"

"Not at all. Anyone who doesn't like you is my enemy too, even if he is my employer."

"I'll be out of everyone's hair soon enough," O'Reilly said. "My job here is finished."

Disappointment showed on her face. "You don't feel like taking another cruise? You didn't really get to enjoy this one."

"That's not a bad idea."

Ted Firestone had returned with Anka's drink, the peach pureé and Prosecco concoction that was the signature cocktail of the legendary bar across the canal and beside him was Benito Buscaglia, Alessandro Martini's private secretary. Buscaglia, looking as obsequious as always, and dressed in a sober, but elegantly tailored gray suit, presumably for the wedding, was clutching a newspaper under his arm. Firestone handed Anka her drink and turned to Buscaglia. "Martini's secretary has some interesting information from the Naples newspaper."

"This was just delivered to me," Benito said. "I want to show it to Mr. Martini. It is a story about you, Mr.O'Reilly."

"Me?" Nothing about O'Reilly had ever in his life appeared in a newspaper and he wasn't at all sure that he was happy that it had happened here in Italy. "What's it about?"

"Read him the title of the article, Mr. Buscaglia," Firestone urged the young man.

Buscaglia unfolded the paper, which was the *Cronaca di Napoli*, the daily newspaper from Naples and spread it out on the table. "The article is called, 'The Cruise Line that Cares,' and it is about Seven Seas Cruise Line." He pointed to the headline, although O'Reilly had no idea what it said beyond what Buscaglia had told him. "It is a story about Mr. O'Reilly saving Marina Stepovich and Helena DeNiro from the Hungarian gang that had taken them to Budapest." He looked down at the newspaper and began to read a part of it aloud. "I am translating," he said.

APPOINTMENT IN MYKONOS

"According to Marina Stepovich's parents
and the two young women themselves, Seven Seas
Cruise Line sent one of its most experienced
investigators, Brian O'Reilly, in search of Marina
Stepovich, not a well-known celebrity or super-rich
passenger, but an ordinary waitress on the *Adriatic
Voyager*. Miss Stepovich and Miss DeNiro, who is
the daughter of a prominent Naples councilman,
had been kidnapped by international sex traffickers.
Mr. O'Reilly not only found the two young women
in the Hungarian brothel to which they had been
taken, but he and other members of the cruise ship
line's security division braved a gun battle with the
sex traffickers to rescue the two young women,
who emerged from the ordeal shaken, but
unharmed. In a time when most of the major cruise
lines are more concerned with concealing the
kidnapping of their crew or passengers and with
denying any knowledge of their being missing in
order to preserve their reputations as safe vacation
destinations, Seven Seas Cruise Line showed itself
to be unafraid to tackle the problem head-on and to
put the safety of its crew and passengers ahead of
publicity. Hats off to Seven Seas employee Brian
O'Reilly and to the Cruise Line's owner, Alessandro
Martini for doing the right thing."

"You're a hero," Anka said, looking up at
O'Reilly with eager, proud eyes.

"They don't know the half of it," O'Reilly
laughed. "I guess Martini won't be unhappy with a
story like that. I'm sure it will frustrate him to see

that I actually did him a favor." He turned to Buscaglia. "Has your boss seen this?"

"Not yet. The paper just came out this morning and I brought it with me to show Mr. Martini, since I know that it will please him."

"Well he's right over there," Captain Firestone said, pointing across the room toward Martini, who, now that the reception line was finished, was heading for the bar, an unhappy and determined look on his face.

"He looks as if he could stand a little cheering up," O'Reilly said. "You know how weddings are. They always make some people cry."

Buscaglia folded the paper and hurried off in the direction of his boss.

O'Reilly turned to his two companions. "Now there's a bit of irony. Martini goes to all that trouble to keep any hint of an abduction off of one of his ships secret, and what does he get out of it? A lot of free positive publicity courtesy of yours truly."

"Looks as if he might have figured that out," Firestone said, his eye on Martini, who was crossing the room on a beeline for the three of them.

When he neared their table, Martini's serious demeanor changed into smiling exultation. "I have misjudged things, Mr. O'Reilly," he said as he reached them. He pulled out a chair next to O'Reilly and sat down. "Benito has shown me the story from the Naples newspaper. You are a hero and we are the most noble cruise line in the world. I was worried about the negative publicity of the press finding out that someone was abducted from my ship and your heroics turned the entire episode into a victory for us all. What can I say? I was wrong. Going after the kidnappers was better than keeping the entire event secret."

O'Reilly leaned back and took a long look at the man. "Don't believe your own publicity, Martini. You had no intention of searching for your missing crew member and if you'd known that she had been abducted, you'd have tried to cover it up just as much as you tried to cover up the fact that your daughter was missing."

Martini shrugged, the smile still on his face. "You are right, of course. But that is why I am indebted to you. You insisted on doing the right thing and look how it has turned out."

"I thought you hated me for forcing you to allow your daughter to marry Sergio."

The ship owner shrugged again. "It is now a fait accompli. I'm not happy with it but my daughter is happy, so I can live with it."

"Bully for you. You're still a first class jerk. Your only saving graces are your daughter and your wife—and now your son-in-law—and the quality of the people you hire... people like Captain Firestone and Anka Sokolov, here, who, by the way is the manager of one of your shipboard restaurants and an up-and-comer you should take notice of." He gave Anka a sidelong wink.

"I see you have taken notice of her," Martini laughed. "You are of course right, Mr.

O'Reilly. Perhaps it is time that I changed my ways." He took a deep breath. "How would you like to come to work for me?"

"How many drinks did you have over at that bar?"

"I'm serious. I am a businessman and I can see something of value when it is in front of me," Martini continued. "You are such a person, Mr. O'Reilly. You did your job well. You asked only for what had been promised you, and you brought nothing but honor to my business."

O'Reilly was skeptical. "So you want me to do what?"

"Why to become Chief of Security for my cruise ship line. I thought that was obvious."

O'Reilly looked at him as if he were out of his mind. Anka and Captain Firestone looked as if they were in shock. "You want me to become the head of your cruise ship security after I blackmailed you?" O'Reilly asked.

Martini chuckled. "As I said, it's a business decision, Mr. O'Reilly. I think that you could be a great asset to Seven Seas Cruise Line. You already have been. You have told me that it is much too easy to cheat in my private gaming room, and you have pointed out that my Security Chief in that gaming room is much too prone to talking about the vengeance he will wreak on people who cheat me out of money."

"The threats are not the real problem. It is that he carries them out."

Martini nodded, turning his chair so that he could speak more privately and lowering his voice. "I agree. I cannot have my employees actually harming my passengers."

"He did more than harm them, he had someone killed. And I'm sure that he was following orders."

"He went well beyond his orders," Martini said, frowning. "Be that as it may, I need to be more sophisticated in how I approach security on my cruise ships and I believe that you are the one who can make sure that that happens."

"You mean no more threats, no more murders?"

"You have my word. I want be a real businessman, not a Mafia or Comorra *duce*. Men like Tony Braga can ruin my business with their methods."

"So Braga would report to me if I took the job?"

"Absolutely."

"I'll think about. Now I'm going to enjoy your daughter's wedding, my friends and this amazing view." He turned his back on Martini.

Martini took his cue and, smiling, stood up and then nodding to the others, left for the table where his wife, his daughter and his new son-in-law had taken seats.

O'Reilly sipped his drink and thought about his life in LA. He still owed rent, and he would still be scrounging for jobs in a culture that was quickly passing him by. The alternative of traveling the ports of Europe and living on a cruise ship was sounding pretty good right now. Even if it did mean working for a sleaze bag.

He looked over at Anka and Ted Firestone. "Mr. Martini has offered me a job as head of security on his cruise line. What do you two think?"

"I still won't let you drive my boat," Ted Firestone quipped.

"And you have to be stationed on the *Adriatic Voyager*," Anka said, looking up at him with a twinkle in her eye, "otherwise what's the point?"

"I see what you mean," O'Reilly answered, feeling as if he was the luckiest man on earth. "So maybe I should take the job…"

He looked back down at Anka and then over at Ted Firestone to see how they reacted. Firestone nodded. Anka pumped her fist.

275

Chapter 45

Captain Firestone stood at the wheel of the Adriatic Voyager, which was still tied up in Venice, and gazed at his old friend, shaking his head, a wide smile creasing his face. "Chief of Security for Seven Seas Cruise Lines, I can hardly believe it. And you took the job! That's even more unbelievable."

"I couldn't resist your fine restaurants," O'Reilly answered. "That and the fact that I will be able to drink as much gin as I want; it will all be free, and I won't have to drive myself home afterward."

"But you'll have to catch the bad guys."

O'Reilly looked down from the bridge of the *Adriatic Voyager* to the decks below. "Where can they go? We're on a floating island. This is the perfect job."

"But it takes a lot more diplomacy than you're used to," the Captain said. "Everyone, even most of your suspects, will be a guest. We can't alienate our guests."

"That's what Tony Braga told me. Of course he had the passenger murdered later when no one was around."

The smile had left the captain's face. "Can you do anything about that? That's not the kind of thing I want to have happen to anyone who comes aboard my ship… not even a cheating gambler."

O'Reilly smiled. "Braga reports to me now. That was one of my conditions and Martini wants Braga reined in. Don't worry, he will be."

Firestone relaxed. "Good. Then you've only got one problem to deal with."

"Anka seems to be fine with my decision."

"I wasn't talking about Anka," the captain answered. "Venice is our last port on this cruise, but we allow the passengers to spend the night on the ship before disembarking tomorrow. We've had some trouble with one of the passengers. He gets drunk every night in the pub and then berates our crew. I didn't want to step in because he was with someone I knew."

"I think I might know who you mean," O'Reilly said, a grin slowly spreading across his face. "The person he's with wouldn't be a pretty woman with big boobs and an urge to hobnob with the rich, would she?"

Firestone grinned back. "That's the one. She tries hard, but you know what they say…"

O'Reilly nodded. "*Once a trollop always a trollop*. But I know just how to handle her boyfriend. In fact, I'm looking forward to it."

Firestone gave him a sharp look, although he was barely able to conceal a sly grin. "We don't want him ending up in a Venice alley with a bullet in his head."

O'Reilly was still smiling. "You mean we *do*, but we know that that isn't what's going to happen."

"Right."

"I'll handle it," O'Reilly said, turning to leave the bridge. "After all, it's my job."

***

Derrick Sterling was already drunk by the time he and Phyllis returned to the ship around ten-thirty at night. They'd apparently eaten in one of the many restaurants in Venice then gone to a bar and had a lot to drink before calling the evening quits and taking a water taxi back to the cruise ship. Phyllis went to bed, but Sterling wasn't going to end his last night on his one and only European cruise so early. He sauntered into the English Pub on the twelfth deck and ordered a beer. When the Filipino waiter brought a ten-ounce glass instead of a full pint, Sterling grabbed the slightly built young man by the collar and began cursing at him for mishandling his order. The cursing soon escalated to denunciation of the man's race and nationality and the bartender called security.

O'Reilly came himself. Alone.

"What the fuck are you doing here?" Sterling slurred, his face revealing his shock at seeing his old nemesis. "I thought we were rid of you. Do you always come to the rescue of one of these slant-eyed chinks?"

O'Reilly turned to the other passengers in the pub, who were looking on with horror. "We apologize for this man's behavior," he said to the other customers. "You can all have a free round on the ship to make up for the inconvenience and

278

embarrassment this man has caused. He will be out of here in a moment."

"What, you can speak for the whole ship now and buy everyone drinks?" Sterling asked, a cruel smile on his face.

"I have a new job. I'm head of the ship's security." O'Reilly smiled back. "And I'm throwing you off the ship."

"You and who else?" Sterling asked, sticking out his chin belligerently.

O'Reilly grabbed the fat lieutenant by his free arm and twisted it behind the man's back, at the same time kneeing him off of the barstool so that he was standing, or rather bending over, one arm painfully pinned behind him. "I guess it will just be me," O'Reilly said. "Just like always." He gave an additional wrench to the man's arm.

"Jesus, OK. Don't break my arm," Sterling whined. He staggered toward the doorway, O'Reilly's knee giving him nudges every time he looked as if he was losing his motivation. When they got to the doorway, the other customers began applauding.

I'm going to love this job, O'Reilly thought to himself.

About the Author

Following along and distinguished career as a research and clinical psychologist, a university professor and dean, and many years of with service in the field of public mental health, Casey Dorman turned to the field of literature. He is the Editor-in-Chief of Lost Coast Review, a quarterly journal of short stories, poetry, book and film review and opinion. He is also the author of the mystery, "Pink Carnation," and the Nyles Monahan mystery series, which includes "I, Carlos" and "Chasing Tales." He is also the author of "Unquity," a literary romance novel and the historical thriller, "Prisoner's Dilemma: The Deadliest Game." Most recently he has authored the satirical political thriller, "Morality: Book One—Where Have All the Young Men Gone?" He lives with his wife Lai in Newport Beach, California.

31174895R00162

Made in the USA
Charleston, SC
08 July 2014